CAUTION TAPE

MOLLY DOYLE
J.D. MIDNIGHT

Cover Design & Title by Opulent Designs

Editing by The Havoc Archives / Autumn Ivy

Formatting & Interior Design by The Havoc Archives

Blurb by The Havoc Archives

First edition 2023

For those who ever wondered what it would be like to give in to your inner serial killer.

Wrap them in plastic first.

Also, don't do it.

Author's Note

This is a erotic horror story about two serial killers. They murder people. They were created to be monsters. With that said, we did not assign any specific mental disorder diagnoses to these characters. We did not want any readers to feel targeted by a diagnosis, or make it seem like people with a mental disorder are inherently evil or violent. Mental health is such an extensive and broad spectrum. It's different from person to person. Any terms the characters may use to describe themselves or each other are not to be taken as indicators for any diagnoses. This is a work of fiction.

Content Warning

abuse of power, animal cruelty, barebacking, biting, blood, blood play, body horror, bondage, bone play, bratting, death, decapitation, degradation, dirty talk, domination, dubious consent, erotophonophilia, fingering, FMF, gore, group sex, hair-pulling, hallucinations, humiliation, impact play, knife play, knives, masochism, mental illness, MF, MFM, murder, oral sex, rough sex, sadism, sexually explicit scenes, spanking, stabbing, strangulation, submission, therapy, violence

Chapter One

Nolan

I am vaguely aware that there is something wrong with me. Something off-kilter and misshapen that defines who I am on a deep level. It projects a barrier between myself and the world. It is invisible to everyone, including me, but I can *feel* it. A certain hollowness. Like the world is a bunch of dry tinder and I'm waiting for it to burn.

Thoughts and feelings occur to me that I know are not the symptoms of a well-adjusted individual, that are not society approved ideations. Everyone has that odd thought when walking on a bridge, right? That flickering, lizard-cold flash of, "*what if I jumped? What if I oopsie-daisied myself into oblivion without a second of introspection? What if I simply gave in to the cold part of my mind?*"

And for a lot of you, it's just that.

A flashing thought.

An odd mood that dissipates the moment your friend starts their next sentence as they walk alongside you. Or the music plays in your headphones. A slight wobble on the big train track of your psyche.

That is where I live. That's my default setting.

For instance, today I am in the community college library, editing a paper for English class. I am twenty-one years old, and I feel lethal. I'm sitting at the computer, changing commas and misspelled words with mechanical efficiency. I'm neither bored nor interested; I am simply there. It feels like a rehearsal. A book I read once described a depressive episode as "it feels like practice." And it does. Everything feels like it doesn't matter very much. Like this brown mahogany desk is secretly made of paper-mâché and can collapse at any moment. As if the skylights of the library complex—all white steel and blue glass—can be swept away in a horrific gust of wind, and me and all the little people will tumble away like leaves.

To my left is a girl from my English class. She keeps glancing at me. I'm used to this. I used to think it was because women could sense the cold lurking inside of me, and then I learned that they liked my confidence, my looks, and the fact that I was nice. I am nice to everyone. It's very easy. My phone regularly buzzes with messages from friends and acquaintances, and I make a mental note to remember something specific about each of them. Jay, for example, likes the Atlanta Hawks. I don't care about basketball, but if I want to deepen my friendship with Jay, I can simply send an Atlanta Hawks joke and he is thrilled.

People just want attention. They want someone to tell them all their little idiosyncrasies are genius. That they are adorable, understood, and appreciated. They want to know that no matter how secretly awful they are, someone will accept them. And if it is handsome, jovial, confident me? Sweet, funny, clever Nolan? Well, that's everything. Who doesn't want pretty people to notice them?

The girl next to me is named Natalie, and three weeks ago she mentioned in class that she had a short story coming out in the student literary magazine.

I turn to her. "Hey, did your story come out yet?"

She blinks twice. She has long, frizzy hair that spills down the sides of her face and bright, heartbreakingly hopeful eyes. She bites her thumbnail, then says rapidly, "Oh, yes. Yes, it did. Do you want to read it? It's on the website."

I know the website. I make a show of typing it into the browser, muttering loudly, "Eerie Community College... slash... what was it? Patterns? Patterns Student Magazine?"

She smiles. "Almost. Rhythms Magazine."

"Ah. Rhythms." I snap my fingers and shimmy my shoulders a little bit, and her smile grows wider. Everyone loves a guy with a sense of humor. I pull up her story and start reading it in front of her. She makes a show of packing up, pretending she didn't know I was going to read it now.

"Wait, God no, please don't—"

I hold up one finger. "Shh, I'm reading."

Is she blushing? Probably.

I read the story quickly. It's a rambling literary piece about summer dying and leaves descending on a young woman as she contemplates the future. I actually sort of like it. It's earnest and very, very college literature. I wonder vaguely if I've ever felt that strongly about anything, to compare it to the collapse of a season.

I turn to Natalie. "I liked it. This spot, right here." I point to the screen. "'Leaves hellbent on hitting the earth, beautiful and suicidal, their destination resolute. I hope I find that. I hope I have the guidance of my individual gravity.'"

Natalie puts down her bag and pulls her chair closer to me. She smells like raspberry hairspray. There's a small mole on her right cheek, just above the corner of her mouth.

I've got her. It was that simple. People are that simple. Give them attention, notice something specific. Remember it. Spit it back at them. Jay and his Hawks. Natalie and her leaves.

All just another rehearsal.

I speak to Natalie for a long time. We go and get coffee. She tells me about her writing struggles. About her ex, the weight of the creative world on her shoulders. I ask questions like, what are you working on now? What do you plan on doing? Do you see anything coming of it?

She gives detailed answers and returns offhand questions to me, which I answer quickly with little detail. She doesn't actually care about my answers, which is fine. People like to have an animated wall to bounce themselves off of, but not something that demands anything of them.

I get Natalie's number. We go separate our ways on the walk from campus. I cross the bridge where I think more of those cold, lizard thoughts. My cell phone vibrates. Natalie is texting me already.

God, it feels thin.

Chapter Two

Cora

It all started when our dog died. Everyone in my family was crying after we found him dead in the living room, saturated in his own filth. His eyes were still open, and his tongue was hanging out of his mouth. Even my father, who had always been a man who kept his feelings to himself, was sobbing from the loss of his best friend.

I, on the other hand, didn't shed a single tear.

I was numb. Confused. Although my body was there physically, I was an empty shell inside, wondering why I was the only one who felt... *annoyed.*

All things die eventually. Death is normal, and it cannot be escaped. We're taught this growing up by the adults we're supposed to trust. Yet, there I was, watching my family grieve while I continued to eat my breakfast at the kitchen table.

And that's when I knew, deep down, that I would *never* be like them.

"You like that?" he grunts, shifting his full body weight onto me, and nearly crushing me in the process. His red face is beaded with sweat. It drips onto my forehead.

"Yeah," I lie, briefly holding up my hands, trying to figure out what to do with them. Where to rest them. Where to touch him.

I sigh.

He sinks into me slowly, fisting my hair as I resume my role of playing a dead fish, frozen in place. Fortunately, he buries his face in the crook of my neck, giving me no reason to force an expression of pleasure.

Once he finishes on my lower stomach, he climbs off the bed in a hurry to collect his clothes from the messy floor. I remain still, lying on my back, waiting for him to find me something to clean up his mess with. He makes no move to do so, instead choosing to retrieve his discarded clothing from the floor.

"Had fun," he mutters, stepping into his pants.

I pause, brow furrowed for a moment as I stare at the wall in front of me. What's his name again?

"Glad one of us did," I mumble dryly, avoiding his gaze as I finally rush to my feet, clearly irritated.

"Can I see you again?"

"Nope," I shoot back, wiping his cum off of me with a dirty sock. "Now get out."

"Whatever," he snorts under his breath. "You look nothing like your profile picture anyway," he quickly adds in, proceeding to exit my room and slam the door behind him as if for emphasis to his point.

Peter. That's it.

No... *Parker.*

Peter Parker? Shit, that can't be right. Whatever.

With that, I climb back into bed unsatisfied and turn off the light, slipping my hand between my legs to finish the job.

"Alrighty. Your total comes to twenty-three dollars and sixteen cents," I casually inform, placing her items into a plastic bag.

"I gave you a coupon," the middle-aged customer snarls. "That should give me an additional twenty-five percent off."

I blink at her.

She grimaces, her eyes turning into small slits. There's a moment of silence between us.

"Well?" she questions rudely. I swallow hard, clenching my jaw tight.

She eyes the nametag pinned to my work shirt. "*Cora,*" she sneers.

"That will be twenty-three dollars and sixteen cents," I repeat.

"I gave you a coupon."

"This total *is* with your twenty-five percent off," I politely explain.

"I'm not stupid."

"I never said you were. The coupon has already been applied—"

She cuts me off, laughing in my face. "Try it again."

"It's already been applied," I say once more.

"What do you know? You're just a girl," she utters dismissively.

I can see the customer behind her roll his eyes.

"I've been around a lot longer than you have, sweetheart—"

"Do you work here?" I interrupt her this time.

She frowns. "Pardon?"

"Do. You. Work. Here?" I slowly let out, ensuring I enunciate to dumb it down for her. "At Target?"

"No."

"Then let me do my job. You're holding up the line," I point out.

"I don't like your attitude, *Cora*. Haven't you heard the saying '*the customer is always right*'?"

"Sure have."

She scowls. "I'd like to speak with your manager," she demands, folding her arms across her chest.

Lauren strolls up behind me right at the perfect time. "Can I help you?" she asks.

"Manager. I *said* I need a manager."

Lauren releases a small, annoyed breath before replying. "You're looking at her," she confirms, opting for a grin. "What can I do for you?"

"Did you hire her?"

"Excuse me?"

The lady shakes her head in frustration. "Cora has been nothing but disrespectful. I'd like an apology from her."

Lauren flashes me an unbothered stare as I pop a piece of gum into my mouth. Amusement flickers in her eyes.

"Cora?" she questions, arching a brow.

"She doesn't believe that I've applied the twenty-five percent off," I tell her. "I've assured her multiple times that I have."

Lauren steps in front of the register with a nod. "Let me take a look," she says, her voice trailing off as she looks over the monitor. After a few seconds, she nods. "Yes. I see it right here. The coupon has been applied, ma'am."

The color immediately drains from the customer's face. For the next several minutes, they go over the numbers in depth until Lauren finally dismisses herself from the register, leaving the bitter old bat to turn back to me with a look of defeat.

"Now, are you ready to pay, Karen?" I ask, leaning forward. "Or are you going to continue being a miserable cunt?"

Her eyes nearly pop out of her head.

I blow a bubble and let it burst right in her face.

Without another word, she hands me a twenty and a five before snatching her bag from the counter and darting toward the doors. I turn to the next customer with a smile.

Chapter Three
Nolan

I'm night driving. Summer is decaying into fall, but the air is still warm. Alive. White moths fly by my windshield, dancing in my headlights as I cruise down the winding, hilly roads that make up the township outside the city.

Pop music thuds through my speakers. There's a breathy, harmonious female voice singing. It's a playlist sent by Natalie. We've reached the "sending each other music" stage of the relationship, which is something I struggle with.

Music does little for me.

I recognize it, I understand it, and I sense the function in most people's lives. But music to me is sugar free soda; it is flat, tasteless, and lacking somehow. I play music out of habit, as a way to find bands and songs that I can use to relate to others. Stockpiling references like ammo for a social battle. Talking to people is a contest to see who runs out of content first.

I switch it off and drive faster, leaving me in a twilight shrouded silence.

I can be my true self at night.

As I continue to drive, I feel the muscles in my face relax. The tightness around my cheekbones, the muscles in my forehead, they all sigh with relief as I drop the amiable, good-natured expression I plaster on my face during the day.

A familiar hollow, dead look greets me in the rearview as I glance into it. When I was a child, the other kids would notice my vacant expression and joke that I was a robot. I had to learn to emote, to manually express things I did not feel. Slowly, gradually, the kids accepted me as normal.

That always bothered me. It was necessary, and sometimes fun, to hide my night self. Though the effort could get exhausting. Being what they wanted all the time took a toll, until eventually the agitation threatened to spill into bloodlust.

So, I night drive.

I drive for hours, letting the lethal waves of rage course through me, feeling every agitation and itch in my hands to strangle, maim, and kill. The ever-present dull ache in my head, the one that makes the world seem vaguely red, rises to a near blinding pain. Even still I drive faster, passing a pickup truck, weaving around a slow minivan, and going deeper into the countryside. All while watching the world outside get darker and darker as the car carries me away from civilization.

On one of the roads, I trail a large Jeep for a while, lost in murderous thought as I watch the red taillights bounce and jostle over each bump.

The rear lights of the vehicle suddenly flair and I hit my own brakes, coasting my car to a rolling stop. A group of deer dash across the road. The Jeep swerves and clips one—the right side of the vehicle slamming into the creature's head.

The Jeep doesn't stop. It weaves around the animal and roars on, ignoring the flailing creature.

I pull over to the side of the road. The other deer glance at their wounded comrade, then dash off, leaving it behind to its fate. It's clear at first glance that the injured beast has a broken neck. It thrashes in the middle of the road for another moment before picking itself up and running clumsily into a ditch. The deer falls before it can get any further, struggling weakly.

I turn off my car and open my glove box. A short, steel knife greets me. I step out of the vehicle, twirling it gleefully in my hand.

I like everything that is happening.

I like the way my footsteps sound on the gravel shoulder. I like the way my arms hang at my sides. I like the way my shirt clings to my body. The knife feels fitted, groomed for my hand.

The grim weight behind my eyes, the constant hunger and boredom, has alleviated for the briefest of moments.

Clarity.

I trudge into the ditch, following the animals' path. The deer is kicking feebly, staring wildly at the sky. One leg is bent underneath it as it lies on its side. Kneeling beside it, I place one hand gently on its ribcage. It shudders and snorts in response. Beneath its warm fur, I can feel its pulse. Rapid. It's in harmony with my own. How long has it been since I've felt my pulse quicken? Since I've felt excitement? Since I've felt any emotion other than boredom and agitation?

I stab the deer twice in the side, the knife eliciting a crunch as it brushes bone and tough sinew. The deer gasps and jerks its head, one of its antlers grazing my left forearm and drawing a gash along the flesh.

Once, some time ago, someone in line at the cafeteria had spilled orange juice on me, and I had to leave the building to stop from chasing them down and kicking them to death.

In this moment though, I am calm. I ignore the deer's struggles and slit its throat.

There's more blood than I expected.

Lovely phrases like "torrent of blood" and "gouts of blood" come to mind as I step back so it doesn't drench me and watch until the crimson spew slows to a trickle.

I've been testing things on different creatures for a while now. Sometimes a hammer. A knife. I dragged an axe over to a coyote mewling on the side of the road once. It's always different than you expect. More blood, or less. The flesh is tougher than you anticipate.

I wonder what it will be like to hurt a human. Will their eyes gush when I drive a screwdriver through them, or will they implode like mini balloons? Can you rip teeth out with pliers, or are the movies lying to me?

A few blissful seconds pass and I watch its eyes roll into the back of its head. Slowly, the thrashing stops.

I'm breathing heavily but my mind is free. The stillness is comforting. It feels like my entire body has uncoiled, as if slipping into a hot bath.

I wipe the knife on the grass and get back into my car, turning on Natalie's playlist and beginning my drive home. Halfway there, I find that I am singing along.

Everyone my age tells me what a nightmare, what a chore, what an awful thing dating is. People are fake, they say. They lie, cheat, and most of all—people play games.

I don't mind though, and dating doesn't bother me. There's a mutual performative aspect to it that I feel very comfortable in. You say cute, funny things. You wear the nice clothes. You slip into the best version of yourself, and then present.

I wish this is all it was. Presentation. Rounded edges. Those little first-date conversations, where everything is isolated and quarantined into what movies we pretend to like, what music and what we're studying at school. If that was as far as relationships went, if friendships only went as far as "Hey, how ya doin'? You see the game last night?" then I might have a chance at that normalcy.

Instead, I'm on manual. Carefully choosing phrases and words to put in my presentation. See my smile. See my eyes. See that I am not hollow and lethal.

Natalie is talking about her project for English class. I'm seated across from her. Around us, the restaurant staff bustles between tables while balancing plates of lobster and steak. They weave around each other while grasping fizzy red alcoholic drinks. It is loud, and my head begins to hurt again.

"—so, the idea is to compare two works of fiction, from two different eras, and show how they are, like, representative of whatever that culture was afraid of at the time," Natalie says, sawing into her steak.

"Do you have two pieces in mind?"

She nods, frizzy hair bouncing. When I picked her up, she'd been wearing a light jacket but has since taken that off, revealing a blue and white polka dot dress. A gold ring on a chain hangs from her neck. As she turns slightly while cutting the steak, I see the writing gleam in the light. She's a Lord of the Rings fan.

My brain catalogs it, enjoying the way it makes sense. It fits. Writer, college student, artsy, Lord of the Rings.

"There's a Shirley Jackson story and a Poe story I want to compare. I think that'll work pretty well. I struggle at finding sources, you know? Like I wish they would just let us have our thoughts instead of needing to cite stuff constantly."

I stop listening and glance down at my arms. I'm wearing a sweater, but I have my sleeves pushed up. The gash the deer left me is red and bright. I caress it gently with my thumb, thinking about the knife.

"What's with the smile?" Natalie asks.

I glance up. "Hmm?"

"You smiled. Like, *really* smiled."

"I smile all the time."

She shrugs. "Sure, everyone does. But normally you don't smile with your entire face. Just your mouth." She gestures to her own eyes. "You smiled just now, with your eyes, too."

I bite my tongue, vaguely amused. She's perceptive, I'll give her that. I glance at the scratch again and feel my "true" smile return. My brain offers something to tell her, and I seize it gleefully.

"I'm just having a really, really nice time with you," I say, thumbing the ridges of the scratch.

Natalie blushes and looks down at her lap. I have the sense the performance is done. Our lines have been read and the audience is satisfied.

Her eyes begin trailing back up to my eyes, probably to say something cloyingly sweet and endearing, when they freeze abruptly on the scratch.

"You're hurt!"

It's her chance, see? She's playing the same game I am, only her desire is to domesticate me into a gently smiling mascot that takes all her moods easily, assures her with constant compliments, wears sweaters and has no problem walking her dog. She's like an alien, wanting to lay eggs inside of me. Use me until I'm drained and vacant, watching sports on the couch while she concocts the next phases of our life that she controls fully.

And it starts with offering care. Simpering, frantic care that proves what a good, doting girlfriend she will be.

My desires are simpler. More... direct.

I want to remove the skin from her skull and run my lips along the smooth, bleached white bone.

"Oh, it's just a scratch. Got it at work. A bit of metal shelving came apart, so we had to bolt it back together."

It's an easy lie. The first of many dead leaves I'll be throwing on the pile. She swallows it easily and gives me another soppy look. It's bright eyed, furious in its intensity. Natalie is thinking I'm perfect at this moment. She's wondering if she needs to start freezing these moments in her mind. She'll need them when she tells 'the story of us' to coworkers, relatives, her social media followers...

If it wasn't so funny, I'd almost be touched.

She started kissing me in the car. She continued to do so on the steps up to the apartment and through the door, her grip on my waist firm, her mouth hungry and forceful on mine.

We trip over a large black and white cat as we move further into the house. She breaks the kiss to cry out, "Sylvester! Move!" before looping her arms around my neck and dragging me back to her bedroom.

My hands are light on her waist as we continue kissing at the foot of her bed, her tongue deep in my mouth. The boredom is back, and I feel a flash of irritation toward Natalie, like her normalcy and humanness has somehow ruined the afterglow of killing the deer.

She breaks the kiss again, dropping down flat from the tips of her toes and tilting her chin up at me.

"Are you okay, Nolan? You don't seem that into it."

I look down at her and feel my irritation growing to resemble real anger. I'm not being normal enough. I'm not an eager, drooling boy. I'm not being human.

Grabbing hold of her wrist, I drop my facial expression, similar to my visage when I night drive. I stop holding up the jovial Nolan mask and let the coldness remove the life from my face.

She blinks twice and her mouth drops open slightly. For a brief, flickering moment, I see fear, and I feel relief.

I'm finally seen.

I'm finally revealed.

Then I realize she's not afraid. Not really.

She's turned on.

"Take off your clothes," I tell her. My voice has dropped an octave and become smoother. I'd read that men with higher voices were seen as deferent and more easily dismissed, allowing me to glide through most social situations without ever being the focus.

In this moment though, I am the focus. There is a certain sense of power in having Natalie look at me that way.

She tears off her jacket and it drops to the floor. Slipping the straps off of her shoulders she then cocks an eyebrow at me.

It occurs to me that she thinks I'm playing a part. A character. She's expecting me to drop the act and dissolve into her arms.

My hand snaps out and closes around her throat, gripping firmly. I pull her in closely, staring into her eyes. Part of me is willing her to see me—truly see me—in all the darkness.

Instead, she gasps, the corners of her mouth curling into a smile.

With one hand still on her throat, I use the other to begin stroking her over her panties. Natalie gasps again, her legs quivering.

"Is this what you want? You want to be treated this way?"

She nods slightly, then breathes the word, "Yes."

I push her onto the bed, her hair splaying out onto the covers, her legs flinging into the air and yelping as she falls back.

Moving over her, I cover her mouth with my palm and use the other hand to rip her underwear off in one smooth motion.

"Shut up," I hiss in her ear. "Shut your fucking mouth."

I straighten up and begin taking off my clothes. Natalie stares up at me but doesn't say anything or move. She continues to watch me until I've taken off my boxers, only then moving to use her legs to hook around my waist and draw me close to her.

"You know, it's interesting," she murmurs, lying on her back, her hands reaching down to stroke my cock. "People have these different personalities during sex. They change into different people." Her hands begin to work faster. "You're different than I expected."

I grab her wrists and pin them above her head, sliding into her roughly. Natalie cries out in astonishment as I pound into her violently. Groaning at the sudden sensation of warmth and wetness, I begin to lose myself. She moans, and my anger flares again. I grab a fistful of her hair as I begin slamming into her harder, drilling her backside into the mattress.

"What did I tell you about speaking?"

Crying out in delight, she grabs onto my arm, her mouth peppering kisses along my neck, chin and lips.

There's a moment, for a while, where I don't think I'll be able to come. My face is pressed firmly against her neck, her hands tightly clasped on my shoulders, sighing each time I sink into her.

I wonder what would be perfect to say to her in this moment. I want to reach into the rancid blender of teeth and knives I call a brain and pull out the wickedness in its most delicious form.

How good would it feel to gasp into her ear, "Last night, I killed a deer. The blood was so warm. No, no, shh... listen to me... it felt *just* how your pussy feels right now."

The thought sends me into a shuddering orgasm. The moan she hears from me is real.

Chapter Four

Cora

My mom started sending me to therapy when I was eleven. She suspected something was wrong with me and believed that me talking with a therapist would turn me into the daughter she'd always wanted.

I was "broken" and she wanted to fix me. She believed I could be *fixed*.

But I'd always wondered if that was even possible.

Since I was a little girl, I've always been different. The black sheep in my family. Even though I'd been numb my whole life, I surely wasn't stupid. I knew that I had darkness lurking inside me.

It turned out that my therapist wasn't cut out for the job. I was immediately referred to a psychiatrist: Michael Burke, M.D. I hated going to therapy, but my mom was persistent. "Talking to a professional will help you," she would say. Too bad they couldn't just shove a bunch of medication down my throat and call it a day. Don't get me wrong, they tried. None of the pills ever seemed to help.

Michael shifts in his chair, resting his ankle over his knee.

"Cora?" he questions.

The loud ticking of clocks drowns out his voice entirely. There must be hundreds of them he has collected over time, hung all over the wall. It's kind of creepy. I chose one and watch it closely, allowing the time to pass. What is time? Is time even relevant? Does everyone experience time the same?

"Is time even real?" I ask aloud, finally turning my gaze to lock my eyes with his.

He rubs his jaw with his fingers. "Do you believe time is real?" he counters.

"I'm not sure anymore."

He nods once, and the moment his lips part, I continue.

"If time is real, then why does the world feel so still?" I wonder, allowing my gaze to settle on the clock once more. "If time is real, then where have I been for the last fifty-eight minutes and fifteen seconds? Sixteen. Seventeen. Eighteen. Nine—"

"You've been here, Cora. In my office. With me," he replies. "Or have you been somewhere else?"

"You lied," I say nonchalantly, pushing myself up from the sofa.

"Did I?" he asks, studying me as he tilts his head to the side.

"You said with therapy, we would figure out why I feel the way I do. Except years and years and *years* have passed, and we still don't have any answers," I reply with mild accusation, slipping my hands into my jacket pockets.

"Perhaps we haven't been asking the right questions," he points out. "Or perhaps there is a part of you that isn't ready for the answer."

Clenching my jaw, I begin pacing the room. "Or maybe there isn't an answer at all. Maybe this has all just been a massive waste of fucking time."

"But is time real?" he challenges.

I snort.

Touché.

"Whether it's real or not," I begin, gesturing to the wall of clocks with a subtle nod, "Time is up."

"Only for today," he declares.

Without another word I turn to leave, feeling his gaze on my backside as I head for the door.

A bright white light invading the room is not the only thing that wakes me from my deep slumber. There's a loud rumble coming from beside me.

Snoring.

You have got to be kidding me.

Slightly lifting my head, I take in the sight of smeared mascara all over my pillowcase. There's a dull throbbing in my skull as I cover my face with my hands, hiding from the harsh morning light. This hangover is no joke.

Fumbling for my phone on the nightstand beside the bed, my stomach gurgles. The din of it is almost louder than the sound of what's-his-names' obnoxious wheezing from beside me.

Right on cue, my head pounds even harder.

I thought my Tinder days were over.

But here we are. Just another night I never got off, and another man who couldn't make me feel the everlasting bliss of an orgasm everyone always raves about.

I told myself that I was done with trying to fill the void inside me with random men. It's never worked before, so what makes me think that it would scratch the itch now?

His snoring grows louder with each passing second. Anger floods through me as I climb out of bed. Everything goes black.

Suddenly, I'm standing over him with my favorite kitchen knife.

I'm going to kill him.

I'm going to fucking *kill him.*

Five.

Four.

Three.

Two—

"Mm," he sighs, rolling onto his side so his back is facing me.

I squeeze the grip of the knife so tightly that all the color drains from my fingers. My heart thuds hard in my ribcage. I can hear the blood pulsing in my ears. Little white dots disrupt my vision, and my head swims.

"Shit," I snarl, reaching for the headboard to keep myself balanced.

"What are you doing?"

I look down at him.

His gaze sets on the knife in my grasp as he scoots to the other side of the bed, staring up at me like I have ten heads. "Woah, what are you doing?" he repeats.

"Leave," I grit out, exhaling sharply, fighting the random burst of dizziness.

He doesn't move.

"Get the fuck out!" I scream, swinging the knife at him as I leap onto the bed. "Get out! Get out! Get the fuck out or I will fucking kill you!"

"What the fuck!" he shouts, bursting into the hallway as I chase after him. "You crazy bitch! Fucking psycho!"

He manages to slip out the front door before I get the chance to bury the blade in his back.

"Shit," I breathe out, gasping for air.

My grip on the hilt loosens and the knife collides with the hardwood. I press my back to the wall beside the front door and shut my eyes, sliding down onto the floor and taking in the euphoric feeling of adrenaline as it consumes every fiber of my being.

Wow.

What a rush.

Abruptly, my eyes shoot open as realization sets in. There's a slippery sensation between my thighs.

I'm drenched.

Chapter Five

Nolan

I awake with a strand of Natalie's hair draped over my face. She's snoring next to me. The room is quiet and serene as I brush her hair away and consider my day. People talk of morning grogginess, of struggling to wake, and not functioning until they have their coffee.

I am not like this. I am simply awake, or I am not.

Instead of sitting up immediately, I gaze at the ceiling.

I could do this.

I could stay with Natalie.

My gaze wanders and I see the pictures on the wall. Hugging someone who is probably her dad. A group photo with friends at a baseball game. Tongue-out, cross-eyed pictures with the cat.

Yeah, I could do it.

We'd settle into peaceful mediocrity. She'd graduate and teach children or work at a hospital. I would work for a car dealership. Maybe a mortgage company, or a real estate firm—something where I could smile and say, "Let's get you into a new house, shall we?"

Our kids would be in sports, or some other kind of group activity. The pictures would pile up. A growing catalog of the grinning, happy family. Photos of vacations and birthday parties. Their first days of school to our third wedding anniversary.

There I'd be, smiling. My kids would look like me and mock my mannerisms, and I would project an image of a doting—if reserved—father and husband. Life would melt away in routine. Natalie would fall in love with each carefully crafted word.

Even still, I'd have my night self. Deer to kill. Rage to unleash.

It excites me a little. The idea of a life-long secret. A grand performance. It sounds like a challenge. Constructing the lie—cementing the house, the minivan, the jobs, the anniversaries and birthdays—and gluing it all into place. Not to mention how the tension of potentially being caught would be delicious.

Because ultimately, one day soon, I want to kill a person. The annihilation of a human being is the next step, but I like to be ready. Mentally prepared. Right now, I feel too impulsive, too fidgety, maybe even prone to impatience. I will make a mistake and all the smiling in the world won't let me get out of it.

Maybe a life with Natalie would teach me that. A thousand movie nights, a hundred PTA meetings, drinks with her friends, all while smiling closed lipped and hiding the teeth of a shark. Yes, that would teach me patience.

She stirs beside me, turning her head to face me. One bleary eye opens. Her voice is thick with sleep.

"Go back to sleep. It's Sunday," she says.

I shift. "Once I'm awake, I don't fall back asleep."

"So serious."

Lazily, her hand drifts down my chest, lingering on my abs, before drifting down further, gently grasping my growing erection and slowly moving her hand up and down, the friction delicious and torturous. She moves closer, kissing my shoulder as she continues stroking.

"You're definitely awake now."

I roll my eyes and she laughs, her breath warm on my neck, her grip firm on my cock.

"I forgot," she says. "No speaking."

She curls up next to me, one leg draped over my thigh. Her lips brush my earlobe.

"But if I talk," she whispers, "maybe that will make you mad. And if you're mad enough..." The pace of her stroking increases, her hand sliding up and down my cock, her thumb brushing the tip with each stroke. "Maybe you'll fuck me like you did last night."

"Maybe," I reply.

I wonder if this was how it happens for people like me. If this was how serial killers and monsters had full, wholesome lives while they secretly maimed and murdered. Did someone just happen to come into their life that at least mildly interested them, enough to stick around for years and years. I imagine myself as a python, languid and aloof, being fed for years, longing to lash out.

I could do the routine. Be in the right spots. My life etched into a spreadsheet. Filled with six o'clock dinners and nine o'clock Sunday Little League coaching. Routine was something to lean on; I could drape my skin over the bones of a schedule and hide for years. The act of assembling a personality to fit that life daunts me.

It just sounds like such tiresome effort.

Natalie's voice interrupts my thoughts.

"Please," she murmurs in my ear. "I want it again. I'm just going to keep talking. I'll talk about anything. Just talk, talk, talk."

I'm not angry. Not really. If I couldn't control my vague, homicidal thoughts, I would have been locked up a long time ago. But Nolan gives people what they want.

I turn my head to stare into her smiling, playful eyes. She thinks I'm still—for the most part—a nice guy. My intensity in the bedroom adds just the right amount of danger to her life. I'm a mirage to her. She'll interact with only the shiny edges, never fully understanding that there is no depth beyond the mirrored image.

Okay.

I slip away from her grasp and grab her arm, pinning it behind her back. Pulling the blankets off her, I roughly push her face down into the pillows. I hold onto the back of her neck as I climb on top of her, trapping her smooth legs beneath my thighs. My chest presses against her as I lean in, moving to kiss down her neck and around the small butterfly tattoo on her shoulder blade. My lips trail down her spine to the small of her back.

She lifts her head slightly. "That didn't feel very angry."

Ignoring her, I straighten up and spread her ass apart, pressing the head of my cock against her folds before sliding in, enjoying the way she moans and arches her head back. I begin rocking my hips, pumping in and out of her with slow, measured strokes.

"Come on, harder."

I gather her hair up into a crude ponytail and pull her head back as I slam into her as hard as I can, her ass pressing firmly against me. I fuck her in rough, violent bursts, my breath coming out in short, harsh gasps as the bed frame creaks and thuds against the wall.

"Little fucking bitch," I growl in her ear, finding myself repeating the phrase as anger and lust have taken over my ability to form sentences. "Little fucking *bitch.*"

She starts to say something, but the words catch in her throat. All she manages is a strangled, hoarse cry, her hands curling the bedsheets as I continue railing her, the veins in my arms popping out as I strain to fuck her harder and harder.

"Oh my *God,*" she cries out and for a brief, surreal moment I think of the knife in my car, and that's when I climax too, groaning with pleasure, collapsing against her with my forehead buried between her shoulder blades.

As I roll off her, clarity hits. Though I'm certain there is very little future for us, for the moment, I am not bored. I suppose that will have to be enough.

Time has passed and I realize I have lost most of the day. This happens from time to time. There's no particular cause or reason; I simply check out. The world passes in front of me, and my face moves mechanically, nodding and talking and moving throughout life, but the swirling force of consciousness that is Nolan is gone. Disengaged. A dark lightbulb. An automaton of flesh.

For whatever reason, when this particular mood strikes me, I tend to wind up at a store. Target. Best Buy. Sometimes a hardware store. Never a grocery store. I need clean, contrasting colors. Sharp red on white tile. Order. The reds and whites bring a sense of calm that I cannot explain, and gliding amongst the little people scurrying around, living their frantic, sweaty lives, brings me back.

I'm in the electronics section. TVs are glowing and flickering like digital eyes. A family is in the next aisle. Four of them: a mother, a father and two boys. The children are hanging off the cart, lolling their pale, blank faces in piggish stupor as they gaze at the shelves. The mother and father are arguing about a TV.

"Will it fit on the wall?" she says.

"Yeah. I can mount it. It comes with these brackets, see?"

"I don't know, won't that hurt our eyes?"

A delicious daydream erupts in my mind. Where I pull a TV off the wall and slam it on the father's head, bashing him over and over, watching blood arch off his skull and spatter the white tile in a bright, vibrant spray. I would hit him, and the TV would fall apart in my hands, chunks of plastic and crystallized glass crunching under my feet. I would change the course of everyone's life forever. I would be akin to a smiling car accident, ripping apart their entire universe in one fell swoop. They would howl. They would scream. They would question the very moral fabric of the world they live in. How could pure, random chance be so malignant to them?

I peer over the aisle divider at them. In nature documentaries they always show a lion peeking over tall grasses at the grazing gazelle. Without warning, the lion leaps at the dumbfounded creatures, sinking bared fangs into soft flesh.

I want to do that.

There's a sudden pain in my hands and I look down to see that I'm gripping the rack of headphones and phone chargers very tightly, as if I'm about to vault over the divider.

I close my eyes.

The urges are getting worse, but for now... I'm still in control. I have time to hone myself into something lethal and discreet. One furious afternoon of biting suburban shoppers is not worth a lifetime in prison.

I walk away briskly, refusing to look back.

On the way out, one of the cashiers asks me if I found everything I was looking for.

I open my mouth to say something nice. Something witty and forgettable, anything to oil what keeps the machine of civil society moving.

Instead, I gnash my teeth and hiss at her, before running out the door into the cold, dark night. The look on her face strikes me as hilarious as I start up my car and drive away, my eyes scanning the road frantically, hoping for another deer.

Chapter Six

Nolan

It is the third hour of men in armor and tree-things fighting each other, and somehow there is yet another movie in this trilogy to watch. My sense of people-pleasing has backfired; I had casually suggested a Lord of the Rings marathon to Natalie just to make her happy. I didn't know they were this long.

I'm having a bad day.

I've observed others having bad days. They drop their keys. Spill their coffee. They blow a tire, or their significant other does something that upsets them. The day is ruined, soured, and they bumble through it like grumpy children.

My bad days start at the center of my forehead, somewhere deep in my brain. A dull ache, like a hunger headache, that slowly slides down and lurks just behind my eyes, pulsing and gnawing.

"Migraines," the doctor called them.

"Migraines," I tell people.

But I know it is something more.

It settles in and makes the world appear a few shades darker. People become distant, shadowy things that I simply don't understand. I seethe with quiet rage and feel disgust at everything living. I consider the fabric of my life and long to tear it apart. Fine, fuck it, blow up the mirage and let the world see the terrible things I want to do to it.

On screen, an elf is talking to a dwarf.

Natalie is next to me on the couch, her bare legs draped over my lap. She is mouthing the lines as the actors speak them.

My hand is on her shin, rubbing it absently. There's a slight dent in the bone, about halfway up. I keep rubbing it with my thumb. Natalie glances at me and smiles, wiggling her toes.

"High school soccer. Accidentally kicked the goal post, broke it, that's the dent."

I smile back.

What if you bite her as hard as you can?

Sink your teeth into the bone. See if your canine teeth will fit in the dent.

Do it, do it, do it.

Leaning down, I kiss her shin gently. "Cute."

Her body vibrates with adoration. But she doesn't reveal it. I have felt her growing more and more attached to me. Every time I remember a little thing about her and mention it again. Every time I kiss some small part of her. Every thoughtful, carefully crafted word is like adhesive, gluing her to me.

She reaches out and grasps my hand briefly. "This is nice," she murmurs, turning back to the TV. "This is *so* nice."

I'm thinking of a scene from a horror movie. A woman with a shotgun brutally executes the people who tortured her, and my mind fixates on how the blood painted the wall after each shot.

"So nice," I repeat.

I manage to get away by offering to go get snacks before we watch the next movie. She groans in mock-ecstasy.

"Why are you the *best*?"

She then lets me go, yelling after me that she's going to take a bath anyway.

I get outside her apartment and I'm suddenly gasping for air, clenching my fists as I walk to my car. It's going to be harder than I thought.

I don't have time to find an animal to kill. I don't have time to night drive and think wonderful, murderous thoughts.

But I can go to Target and glide amongst red-lined aisles and blissfully, cool white tiles.

The automatic doors are reassuringly smooth as they slide open to greet me. It is late evening on a Tuesday. There is pop music playing above me as I swim through aisle after aisle of candles, picture frames, mirrors, and the occasional beanbag. The store is mostly empty, and I am the lone ghostly figure, wandering around and thinking my exquisitely dark thoughts.

It is frustrating to have them categorized that way. I don't find them dark. I don't find them frightening, heinous or anything else of that nature. Other people do. The little shadows that flit around me are so easy to scare and manipulate.

I don't know why I play their game, other than it is easy and I am good at it.

I come out of my thoughts in the kitchen aisles, at the rows and rows of glossy knives, meat hammers, cleavers and cutting boards. I run my hands along them, each new tool bringing a flashing scene of bloodshed to my mind.

A serrated steak knife.

Dragging it across her skin. Watching it snag and tear.

The long, seven-inch Santoku knife with the stainless-steel handle.

Driving it into her stomach.

Would it pop like a balloon? Would all the air rush out as it deflated?

Tiny paring knives. Two of them in a set.

What sound would she make if I stabbed her? Would she choke? Would she groan? Would she SCREAM?

"We're closing."

The voice is cold, haughty, and seemingly pissed off. I turn to my right and look down slightly to see an employee in a red polo shirt and beige capris glaring at me. Her arms are folded, and her nails are painted black, though I notice they're chipped, almost as if she enjoys picking at them. Studying her features, I take note of her dark, faded blue eyes. They could almost be gray. They're starkly contrasted against the black bangs framing her face, her short hair shining with the stinging brightness of the fluorescent store lights. I enjoy the way her mouth moves as she bites the inside of her cheek, like she's resisting the urge to say something mean.

"Closing already?" I ask. "You're gonna make me go home? Really?"

Her eyes narrow to small slits.

I flash her my smile with the expectation that the attitude will drop, absently expecting the anger to dissipate slightly. I let my eyes drift down her body, and I make it obvious, tilting my chin up and down in an exaggerated manner. Her name tag reads "Cora".

"We close in five minutes." She shifts her weight to her other foot and somehow manages to harden her glare further. "Please leave."

Interesting.

She didn't react to me. She's attractive, absolutely, and sometimes attractive people put up a front and have this aloofness to them, even when coming across someone who looks as good as I do. But that's not the impression I get. Cora from Target looks genuinely disgusted by the mere fact that I exist.

There's a brief pause before I respond, my hand still near the paring knives. Meeting her eyes, I find myself gauging what kind of new creature is standing before me, when she breaks the gaze for the most minute moment.

She glances at the knives in that same lustful, hungry way that I do.

Smiling slightly, I walk out of the aisle. Sparing a glance over my shoulder as I leave the store, I see Cora trailing her fingers along the racks of knives, a dreamy and distant expression on her face.

I'm still thinking about her as I drive back to Natalie. It is only halfway there that I realize I forgot to grab snacks.

The days begin to take a toll on me.

I watch them roll on, a series of Thursday the fifths melting into Thursday the twelfths; my sense of time becoming a flowing, tangled sequence of images.

Dinners with Natalie, her face breaking apart and becoming Cora's as my mind drifts lazily around, testing out different fantasies to keep itself entertained. I pick up hours at the hardware store just to occupy myself, and the steady, high-pitched *bee-woop* of the cash registers start to calcify in my brain, making me grit my teeth as I take inventory. It gets to the point where I hear it even when I'm in the backroom, amidst stacks of bird seed and legions of gleaming riding lawn mowers.

Bee-woop.

Now it's Monday.

Bee-woop.

Friday. I'm losing days.

Bee-woop.

I'm still in the store, and a customer is talking to me. An old man with a white halo of hair circling a liver-spotted bald scalp that shines under the fluorescents.

He's asking about extension cords and my mouth goes dry. I'm looking deep into his runny, watery green eyes, the word "cord" sticking in my head.

Bee-woop.

"We have some of the waterproof ones in aisle nine," I tell the man. "Orange ones, all on the rack."

“Thank ya, thank ya,” he says. He totters away from me, shuffling along the rows of gardening tools and weed wackers.

His eyes would bulge so sweetly if I wrapped that orange *cord* around his throat. The *cords* in my arms would stand out as I pulled both ends so fucking hard that the rubber insulation would dig into his flesh.

Would his head pop off? Would it pop off like that little fucking piggie that went wee-wee-wee all the way home?

A thin line of drool leaks out of my mouth and rests wetly on my chin. I sway on the spot, a dizzying impulse to run after the old man on all fours and kill him in front of everyone. I could drag him by the neck to the checkout lines, screaming “BEE-WOOP! BEE-WOOP!” as I smashed a register onto his head, over and over and over—

and over and—

red rover, red rover, send Nolan right *over.*

Bee-woop.

The checkout line goes off again, and it snaps me out of it like a smelling salt waved under my nose. I retreat to the backroom and place my forehead on one of the cool, smooth bags of bird seed.

I manage to get through the work shift without committing homicide. There were plans to meet Natalie for a movie, bowling, or perhaps a card game night with her friends—something like that.

My phone hasn't stopped blowing up with notifications all day. I should have turned it off but on some level, I was enjoying the escalating rage. In contrast to the hollow feeling, it was nice to burn with a churning, heinous feeling. Even if it made life increasingly difficult to handle.

I finally take the time to check my phone as I leave the store and see that she sent me a picture. A small, woodcut sign with etched stars and sparkles on it that says, 'in this house, we believe in magic'. Another message is right under it.

Natalie: Maybe I should put this above my bed after last night ;) That WAS magic.

I sit quietly in my car for a moment. I feel feverish, a clammy seasickness at the very act of existing. After staring blankly at her text message for a long time, I somehow manage to open my car door and vomit onto the sidewalk.

Oh, Nolan. You used to be so in control.

I start the car and begin driving, with no destination in mind, just the visceral need to be on the move.

I'm still driving when the radio begins speaking to me.

It's one of those talk radio shows. Two grating voices going back and forth—and what do you know—the reliable American subject comes up.

Serial killers.

"How do you not notice?" the gravel-voiced host says. "You know, you live with a guy for years—years! And you *never* notice he's hiding bodies in the basement? Sticking bones in the walls?"

"What I want to know is where these guys get the type of wives that'll leave them alone that long," the sneering, higher pitched host replies.

"Thank you! I can't get through a playoff football game without hearing it from my wife, meanwhile John the Axe Murderer has a house of corpses, and his wife is like, "Well he works late sometimes and has his hobbies—"

"He's a little quiet sometimes—"

"A little distant—"

"A little weird in bed—"

"Ha! You ever wonder what these guys do in bed?"

They go on, but I tune them out as I rotate that particular unique phrase in my head.

House of corpses.

Here are the bones, laid neatly in the floorboards.

Here is the gray, cold flesh encased in cement.

Don't forget the heads tucked neatly in the rafters of the attic.

I can see it in my mind's eye, a house with black shutters and white peeling paint, filled to the brim with bulging flesh, limbs and meat and eyes all tumbling out of the windows and doors. They're oozing out in a mass of pink and red, like Playdoh pushed through a cookie cutter.

I need to get started.

The plan to build a camouflaged nest of a life won't work if I snap and assault someone in public. I'll need to kill and move, kill and move. I would be caught, eventually. I could picture it, faceless shadows pinning me down as I shriek at them. All the while knowing gleefully that they're in for years' worth of backtracking and digging up bodies in every corner of the map. My house of corpses—built only as a grim metaphor. I must first begin with the foundation, my basement.

My first kills.

My aimless driving ends abruptly as I realize I've driven back to Natalie's house. There are lights on in the living room and I see shadows moving. I take three deep breaths and begin testing out different faces to wear. Different smiles, different forlorn looks, even different inflections of the eyes. I'm not going to be able to hide that I'm struggling with something; I don't need to. I just need to make it into something she can understand, something she can sink her teeth into, that allows her to feel like a good girlfriend as she solves her emotionally stunted boyfriend's problems.

Oh, no, it was one of those days, you know? Where you wonder what you're doing with your time. With your LIFE. Ever have that? A little existential crisis during the work shift. You ever have that, babe? Sweetie? Honey?

She'll take me in and give me a glass of wine and sit cross-legged on the sofa and listen to me complain, nodding her head in understanding. She'll deliver some somber advice about finding yourself, your *real* self, and that'll be that. All while swelling with that sense of *doing good*, and I'll keep fucking her until something more interesting comes along.

I walk up to her door, the porch creaking and shifting after each step. *House of corpses* flares up in my mind once again, so that when she opens the door, I'm smiling for real.

Chapter Seven

Cora

My deepening anger at the world intensifies over the next few days. I've always been told that something is wrong with me. That I need help. It's been drilled into my head for so long now that I've almost started to believe it.

Almost.

Until my encounter with Tinder guy, when I chased him through my apartment with a knife in a fit of rage. That was the first time I've felt truly alive.

These last few days, I've been chasing that same high ever since. I've always experienced dark thoughts. Intrusive thoughts, Michael calls them. Except, to me, they weren't intrusive at all. They felt normal. They felt right. Except I've always been warned to never act on those impulses, and now I realize it's because they could get me into a lot of trouble.

"It's open," I call out after hearing several knocks at the front door.

Jerald casually strolls into my apartment dressed in jeans, and a baggy hoodie, along with his usual black beanie. He's the only person in my life who I would consider an actual friend. My inability to connect with people makes it almost impossible to have real friendships. Relationships of any kind, really.

But with Jerald, it's easy. He doesn't ask questions and doesn't expect anything from me in return. He's different.

"What are you supposed to be?" he wonders, looking me over.

I shrug, glancing down at my tightly fitted black dress and black boots that end just below my knees.

He grins. "Well, whatever you are, you look good," he tells me.

"Thanks," I say dismissively, brushing the knots out of my hair with my fingers. "I'm not finished yet."

Jerald plops onto the couch and entertains himself with his phone. I grab the bottle of fake blood from the table and squirt some onto my finger, like toothpaste on a toothbrush. A warm sensation rushes through me, traveling all the way down my body as I smear some of the blood on my chest, staring at my reflection in the mirror plastered on the wall.

My heart beats wildly at the image.

Suddenly, I'm smearing the entire container of blood all over me, bathing my arms, neck, and chest in the red liquid.

"Jesus, Cora," Jerri mutters. "You think that's enough blood?"

I lower my gaze to the hardwood floor, noticing the stray droplets that have somehow trickled onto it. Grinning, I stare at my crimson stained palms and fingers. My hands are cold though, and my smile quickly fades.

"Ready?" he asks.

"Yeah," I answer, trying to imagine how it would feel if this were real blood instead. It would be warmer. Inviting. The knife I've stored in my boot calls out to me. "I've never been more ready."

Nolan

It is Halloween and I know who I am going to kill.

During class I read article after article, page after page about serial killers and madmen, tons of which kidnap and slaughter women, only to get caught somewhere down the road. It never seemed to matter how clever and devious the killer was.

Serial killers always have a myriad of reasons and motives for why they do the things they do. Their mothers abused them. The devil whispered to them. God had his orders.

I don't like those ones very much. Some of us simply feel like killing.

From my time studying I noted that men seemed to be much easier to kill.

They are often less social. They can disappear for a few days before people start asking questions. They can stop responding to messages or appearing online, and it'll be longer before the world notices. It is normal for men to go places alone, without telling someone where they're going. They walk with security that nothing bad is likely to happen to them.

But I am something bad.

Jerald Clarke thinks he's been messaging a 5'4" brunette off a dating app. He thinks they're meeting at a Halloween party thrown by the business club at the school. It has taken weeks of urging, coaxing, and teasing to get him to agree to come out. He goes to the same college, and I've even seen him in the halls, curly brown hair stuffed under a beanie and an overgrown beard. He's what Natalie calls a "skater type", which makes sense, I guess.

I personally have never spoken to Jerald Clarke, and I have taken measures to make sure we are never seen together at school. A carefully planned measure so that when the police come asking, if they even get to me, it'll be very easy to say, "I've seen him in the halls, but never spoken to him."

Perhaps they might see that he's been messaging a fake account on the app, and if they try to trace that account it'll show an IP somewhere in eastern Russia, with a dead email account attached.

That's if they find the body.

"We'll meet dressed up," I text him. "It'll be exciting."

Jerald texts in all lower case and misspells words to be cute. He sends too many kissy face emojis. It makes me want to stab him to death.

Natalie is thrilled that I want to go to the party. When I mention matching costumes, she slaps my shoulders and shrieks, "Yes! Oh my God, I have so many ideas."

Now I'm at a loud, sloppy Halloween party thrown together by people who are barely old enough to drink. It's a house party, with people milling around the large living room, drifting in and out of the kitchen, making drinks on the dining room table. People clustered together and are talking too loudly despite being so close to one another. There's a smell; like sweat and spice in the air, and it makes my nose itch. An annoying mix of Halloween songs and rock music are playing from a staticky stereo system.

I let Natalie lead us around, talking to random people she knows from class. We are dressed as Gomez and Morticia Addams; I am wearing a striped suit with a red tie and mustache drawn on with mascara. Natalie is fitted in the mermaid style black gown that Morticia classically adorns, her hair dyed black and straightened, her face powdered pale. She pulls me by the hand around the house, and I let her, making sure everyone sees us.

If someone were to be questioned later, they would merely reply, "Nolan? Yeah, he was with Natalie all night."

We play a board game for a bit, and I keep fetching Natalie drinks. Before long, she's bumping into me when we walk and giggling at everything. We're sitting cross-legged around a dented coffee table, game pieces, cards and drinks strewn in front of us. We're playing against a vampire, two guys dressed as the Joker, and a very loud woman in a leopard-print cat costume.

Normally I'd want to leave or drive my car through the building and hear their bodies thud off my car. Before that thought goes much further though, my phone vibrates, and I sneak a glance at it.

Jerald: I'm here baby!

Jessi: I'll be there soon. My skirt is shorter than I expected ;)

I put the phone in my pocket, and within seconds it vibrates as he answers back. That message will keep him at the party for a long time. Long enough to get Natalie home. Long enough to change.

Someone rolls the dice and I absently play a card. Natalie is chattering next to me with one of the Jokers.

The front door opens and Jerald wanders in, not in costume, just an overly large hoodie and his usual beanie. I take notice of him and turn back to the game; if I need to, I can always send a message from "Jessi" that'll keep him here for as long as I need.

An hour slips by, Natalie has two more drinks. The Jokers leave, new people arrive at the party. Natalie and I wander into the kitchen, talking about horror movies.

Jerald is there. He's talking to a girl in a black dress that clings to her very well, accented with black boots that stop just below her knee. She's covered in fake blood.

"I'm supposed to meet Jessi here," he's saying to her, "but I feel like I'm going to get stood up." I open the fridge, pulling out a bottle of water, and hand it to Natalie, who is twirling in a slow circle and talking about Scream 4.

The girl turns slightly, and I feel a twinge of shock; it's the girl from Target. The cute one with murder in her eyes.

Cora leans against the kitchen island and shrugs. "She'll be here. You're a good guy. I'm sure she's excited to meet you."

I'm nodding and murmuring back at Natalie while I eavesdrop. I can't place the reasoning, but I find that it kind of annoys me that Cora is friends with Jerald.

"Right, right," Jerald says, waving the cup that's in his hand, "but who wants to meet at a Halloween party for the first time? In costume? What?"

I can hear a hint of malice and boredom in the undertones of Cora's voice when she replies.

"Some people like to do exciting stuff. Life is so fucking boring. Wait, where is your costume?"

Jerald grins and pulls out a cheap, flimsy Zorro mask, and slides it over his head.

"What do you think?"

"Oh, that's *real* sexy, Jerri."

Jerri? Why does *that* annoy me?

Natalie is suddenly on me, wrapping her arms around my waist, pressing her hips against mine. Her mouth trails up my neck and she begins kissing me.

"Gomez, take me home," she mumbles.

I steal a quick glance at Cora and Jerri as we leave the kitchen. Cora looks at me and I see a flicker of recognition, but Jerald is saying something else, and she turns back to him.

Chapter Eight

Cora

The guy I saw the other night in Target is here. *Why* do I remember him? What makes him so memorable?

Maybe it's the way he seems to carry himself. It triggers something inside me. He's much too confident and good looking, and he knows it. He is just another conceited man who believes his shit doesn't stink. But in reality… he *reeks*.

Although, he doesn't reek of normalcy like most people. When I look at him, it's like catching a glimpse of myself in a mirror. He reeks of deceit.

Target guy exits the kitchen with a girl who clings obsessively at his side. She sparks a feeling of distaste in me. I could never understand girls like her.

Truthfully, I will never understand people in general. I try to.

Sometimes.

I'm never able to find anything in common with anyone. It feels as if nobody shares the same feelings about the way I happen to view the world around me.

"You good?" Jerri asks me.

I meet his gaze and shrug. "I'm fine," I reply.

"Do you know him?" he questions, arching an eyebrow, eyes filled with suspicion.

"Who?" I ask, tossing back a shot of vodka.

"Never mind." He lowers his gaze to the screen of his phone and sighs. "I can't wait to meet her."

"Who?" I ask absently.

"Jessi..."

"Oh. Right."

"I'm actually kind of nervous," he admits with a laugh.

"You'll be fine. I'm sure you both will meet and then live happily ever after."

He laughs again. "That would be nice."

"You'll become the best of friends. Move in together. Get married. Have a baby. Have some more babies," I mutter dryly while pouring myself another drink. "Before you know it, you'll be celebrating your thirtieth anniversary and looking back at your mundane life wondering where the hell all that *time* went and how it all went to shit in the end."

He's staring at me with a look of disapproval when I meet his eyes.

"Well, fuck, Cora," he mumbles, taken aback. "I don't even know how to respond to that. That was—" Hesitating, he nervously gulps down the rest of his beer. "That was really depressing."

"It's the truth, Jerri."

"You should really just keep some thoughts to yourself."

I frown. "Why?"

"Because you come off as cold sometimes."

"So what?" I ask, leaning against the counter. "I am cold. That's just how I am."

He rolls his eyes and devotes his attention to his phone. "Whatever, Cora. Appreciate your words of wisdom."

"Would you rather I lie to you?" I question. "Tell you that life is beautiful? That what's meant to be, will be? That everything happens for a reason?" He stays silent. "Yeah. That's what I thought."

"Hi there, pretty lady," a voice interrupts us. I feel them place their hand on my shoulder, causing me to spin around and snatch his arm, twisting it behind his back. My voice is low next to his ear as I tighten my grip, nails digging into the soft flesh of his wrist.

"Touch me like that again and I'll peel your face off to use as my next Halloween mask. Capiche?"

He lets out a small gasp as I give him a shove across the kitchen.

A few people laugh. Others just stare.

"As strange as you are..." Jerri eventually says. "Never change, Cora."

"I don't plan on it. Now let's go dance."

Nolan

Natalie has been talking all night about how hot it'll be to fuck in our costumes, but by the time I half-carry, half-push her into her bed, she's asleep. I take her shoes off and cover her carefully with the blanket. If she's comfortable, she'll sleep longer, giving me more time to be away before she wakes up and notices.

I strip the suit off and dress in a black long sleeve shirt and jeans. In addition, I have gloves, a black mask, and a long, thick rope.

My hands are shaking with excitement by the time I get to my car, and my heart is hammering in my chest when I finally get back to the party. I opt to park down the road away from streetlights. Reassuringly, the ache in my head is completely gone.

There is a wonderful sense of clarity and purpose. The world has simplified into a very narrow corridor. I have one goal, one objective, one desire.

Kill.

I send another message.

Jessi: I'm lost. Could you come outside and wave so I know which house it is?

Jerri, of course, obliges.

I watch from the shadows as the door opens and Jerald ambles out, laughing with someone from inside, before closing the door and descending down the steps, his eyes on the blue-white glow of the phone.

Jessi just can't find the street.

Jerald begins strolling down the sidewalk.

Jerald: I'll walk up and down the road. Let me know when you see me!

He passes my car as I pull on the mask and shrink down in my seat. He's still tapping away at his screen. I slip out carefully and glide along the length of my car behind him, cursing my footfalls on the concrete and hoping he doesn't hear.

Somewhere in the distance a cat yowls.

Without warning I'm behind him, looping the rope around his neck and pulling it as tight as I can. A yelp catches in his throat, swiftly turning into a choked gargle. His hands attempt to beat the side of my face as he flails backwards, but I pull tighter. His hands jump to the rope instead, desperately trying to dig for separation. I catch his scent while his hair drifts into my mouth in the struggle, smelling like beer and weed. He's heavier than I expected, but he's still going to die.

I drag him backwards toward my trunk. His body sags, legs going limp and parallel to the ground. Hauling him up I fumble to open my trunk with one hand while squeezing the rope with the other.

I have to get better at this.

As the thought arcs across my mind, Jerri coils his legs and pushes backwards, flinging himself into me and making us both fall. Bouncing off the car's bumper we land in a heap on the pavement.

The groan he emits is a half-wheeze and he scrambles to his feet, setting off on a tottering run, hands outstretched to the light of the house. To the party, and safety.

It's a fair attempt, but I'm much faster.

The rope is back around his neck. This time all he can manage is a weak cry of, "Please?"

Then his head droops, he stops struggling, and it is delectably easy to tip him into the trunk and drive away.

I'm feeling so much better.

There's an alacrity to my thoughts, a crisp cleanness, like each synaptic connection is super-charged. How good a feeling, to begin the assault on a fortress of an idea after years of contemplation. Of building and amassing yourself for the attack.

It is about to happen. I am about to become a serial killer.

The headaches have subsided, and the loose, frayed sensation of reality has been replaced by a deadly—almost delirious—focus.

Things are going wrong, sure, but I handle them with gentle efficiency. Almost like an aging husband dutifully caring for his elderly wife near the end of her time on this earth.

Jerald struggles when I pull him out of the car and drag him to the shipping container, so I beat him until he's still, the blows landing with flat, muffled thuds in the chilly night.

He's too heavy to haul onto the table, and that's disappointing. I tip him into a rusted folding chair that I'd found during my various excursions around the shipyard.

Using bike locks, I bind his wrists and ankles to the chair. He's loosely conscious, mumbling incoherently. When the last lock snaps closed around his left ankle, he jerks awake and screams.

I stand up. "I will keep hitting you if you don't stop."

His head droops and he spits out one of his teeth.

"Unh," he groans, then clears his throat.

I drag one of the totes over to him and begin rummaging through it, delicately placing tools at his feet. A hammer, a screwdriver, and a wicked looking pair of gardening shears.

Finally, a brand-new nail gun, the smell of the orange plastic still fresh and chemical.

I sit cross-legged at his feet, looking up at him and I smile. "I'll be honest, I'm feeling kind of shy. I've never done this before."

"What—what are you talking about? Just fucking let me go. Let me go right now. Right now. Right now, please."

I shake my head. "No, I'm not going to do that. I'm going to hurt you. Very badly. But I've never killed anyone and I'm a little overwhelmed." I gesture around at the plastic sheeting on the floor, tacked to the metal walls. There's a gleaming steel table off in the corner, and totes of supplies. A rust spot looms on the wall to my left, like an old bloodstain, and I find it comforting. "I've killed some animals. Deer. Squirrels. Can't kill dogs or cats, you know, people notice that."

To his credit, Jerald seems to have some courage in him. A certain dignity. He shifts in the chair, struggling to straighten himself. I watch his jaw tighten, the mole on his chin standing out as his brown eyes flicker around the room. I can almost hear his brain whirring as it struggles to put together a plan.

Keep him talking, he's thinking. *Keep him talking and he'll slip up. Keep him talking and the police will arrive. Someone saw him kidnap you. Someone knows you're gone.*

I have his phone. I reach over to plop his index finger on the sensor and open it. I scroll through and to my delight find that he has his credit cards saved to it. He has a few missed messages, including one that asks if he was still interested in buying a car.

"You don't have a car?"

"Wha—no." He realizes too late that giving me information isn't in his best interest and falls silent.

"You're making this too easy." I buy a few tickets for a music festival in another state, then post on his Facebook, "I got tickets for Horizon Fest! Getting out of town for a few days, fuck yeah!"

I show the post to him. He frowns. "My friends won't believe that."

Shrugging, I turn the phone off. "It'll fool the police for a little while. If anyone even notices you're gone." I scratch my head, before looking back down at my tools. "You ever turn on the TV to watch a movie, and all the choices you have kind of paralyze you? You want to watch everything and nothing all at the same time. If you pick a horror movie and it's bad, well, you wasted that time you could have been watching something better. Trust me, there's always something better."

"Look dude, if you let me go, I'm not telling anyone. I'll say someone tried to rob me. I didn't see their face. I won't tell, I promise. I sell drugs, alright? Just weed and some Adderall but like, come on, I don't want to talk to cops."

I ignore him. I'm mostly talking to myself. "What I've found is that you simply have to pick fast. Can't linger. Gotta pick something immediately." I snatch up the hammer, twirl it once in my palm, and then slam into the top of Jerald's knee. I do it with the gleeful joy of a kid hitting the Test Your Strength game at a carnival. I do it so hard that I can imagine the bell rising up-up-up, making the lights go ding-ding-ding and I win all the prizes.

Jerald makes a lot of noise. His screams are clipped and hoarse, sounding more like disbelief than pain. They remind me of an alarm clock. "Ah! Ah! Ah!"

I lean in close and can smell a greasy, acrid scent. Fear-sweat, an odor like old socks intermingled with that metallic scent batteries give off. Hanging his head, his hair falls wetly across his face. His chin presses against his chest as he gasps for air. He's trying to control the pain.

I let him rest for a long pause, at least until he looks up again. The moment he meets my eyes, the hammer arcs through air and hits the other knee. The vibration of it goes up my arm. A wet *crunch,* not unlike biting into breakfast cereal, emits from his kneecap. The fabric of his jeans rip, and blood begins to well; a small volcano erupts out of his knee.

He bursts into frightened, childlike sobs. A thin, gleaming line of snot dribbles out of his nose, mixing with the tangle of facial hair on his upper lip. His entire body shakes, like he is being ravaged by a fever. He begins a desperate, blubbering plea. "Please. Please, puh-lease don't do this—"

I zone out a little. There's a plastic trigger guard on the nail gun that I can't get off. It's one of those thick, impenetrable zip ties. I try to break it off, but I can't get enough leverage. I pick up the screwdriver, but it just scratches the nail gun and gets wedged between the trigger and zip-tie. I pull it out and toss it to the side and give Jerald an exasperated sigh. "Nothing's ever simple, is it?"

"Let me go, let me go, let me go—"

"STOP ASKING FOR THAT!" I shriek, dropping the nail gun, letting it crash and clatter on the ground. I lunge at him, seizing his face in my hands and tilting it up to me. Closing my eyes, I attempt to collect myself.

"I am not going to let you go," I tell him, gently, like he's my student who simply doesn't believe in himself. "If you do not stop, I am going to see how many nails your balls can take before you pass out."

His words cut off abruptly in his throat, his eyes bulging. I see a bit of blood leaking out of the corner of his mouth; he's biting his tongue to keep from making noise.

I return to the nail gun. After some twisting, the zip-tie pops off. With trembling hands, I load a rack of long, silvery nails into the slide mechanism and rack forward. I wonder if this will become something I do to all my victims, or if it's a once in a while thing like when the mood strikes me.

On Thursdays, it's nails. Saturday's chainsaws.

I'm musing on this, fiddling with the tool, when Jerald interrupts.

"Is this about Cora?"

I glance at him. That mole catches my eye again resting just above his chin; I can see it underneath his beard. It moves with his face, a jostling brown dot that jumps and quivers.

He's still talking. "You were watching her at the party. It's fine, I'm not interested, really, go ahead bro—hey—hey—WAIT—"

I jam the nail gun flush against his chin. I push it upward, like an electric shaver, the plastic prong guards on either side of where the nail comes out rasps against his facial hair making a crinkly sound that bothers me more than I would imagine, but it makes me feel justified.

When I squeeze the trigger, something fascinating happens.

First, the nail blasts through his flesh and wedges halfway into his jaw. The *thwack* of the gun firing and the sickly *galuck* sound of the metal splintering bone sends a delicious thrill down my spine, and I can't help but groan in delight.

It went in *so* deep.

And Jerald! Look at him go! It's akin to when fish get pulled out of the water, how they jerk and twist and flop. Well, Jer-Bear can't twist and he can't flop, but oh baby, can he jerk! He positively *vibrates* with pain, his head whipping back and forth while rocking the chair sideways so hard I have to catch him from tipping over. Blood, bright and glorious blood spurts out in chaotic, frequent splats. It bursts, like the blood is speaking in Morse code.

I watch as he grips the sides of the metal folding chair so hard that his fingernails show cracks, splintering on the curved metal tubing, blood leaking out from under his cuticles.

I step back for a moment, wanting to savor it. To examine it from all angles, this suffering wrought before me.

The shipping container creaks. A small, slight metallic groan that is obviously a gust of wind making the container shift, but that fact doesn't stop a sudden, paranoid—yet tantalizing—idea.

A fantasy hits me like hot water is poured over my head.

Cora, in that black dress, catching me in the act with Jerald.

I imagine Cora, striding toward me and glaring as I shrug helplessly. Stopping an arm's length away, she leans down, her hair falling in front of her eyes. Slim fingers work along her hips to the hem of her underwear, slipping them down long legs and stepping out of them with dainty precision. Then as she turns around, she bends over in front of me, tight dress riding up around her hips. With a smirk, she moves to place her panties delicately on the exposed nail that is artistically penetrating Jerald's face.

As if she were hanging up a coat.

Jerald gags, breaking the fantasy and bringing me—regretfully—back to earth.

"I don't have Cora," I tell him, and I get the sense he's not really listening. "But I do have you!"

The next nail *does* go into his balls, and what do you know, that fish *can* jump.

Chapter Nine

Cora

Target Guy drove down the street, taking a sharp turn, disappearing into the night. He didn't see me lurking in the shadows, and I assume he believed he was alone. Except he wasn't.

I saw it all, and I know Jerri is with him.

In the trunk.

I try to wrap my head around what I just witnessed. So, Nolan isn't normal after all, just as I had suspected. That normal façade isn't correct. He has layers… how interesting.

Instead of screaming for help that my friend has just been choked out with a rope and shoved into a trunk, I stroll down the sidewalk and casually make my way back into the Halloween party.

I fetch myself another drink and play out a few different scenarios in my head. Maybe that girl Jerri has been talking to—Jessi—has set him up. Maybe this is some kind of kinky role play that he found himself a part of.

For a moment, I become fascinated just thinking about the idea of it. At least until I freeze, half choking on my drink as the booze drips down my chin and neck.

What if there is no Jessi?

What if there *never was*?

I ponder why Target Guy has taken him and I wonder what exactly he has in store. What his plan is or even what the end game goal could be. Abruptly, I find myself smiling with anticipation.

For the first time in a long time, excitement consumes me.

I'm going to find out.

Nolan

"A guy from our school is missing," Natalie tells me one morning. She is sipping orange juice and flipping through an actual newspaper; one of those little eccentric routines of hers that she claims keeps her "grounded" and "rooted in reality."

I don't care, but she's flipping the newspaper pages self-importantly, peering down the nose of her reading glasses—that I don't think she actually needs—and clucking her tongue. Normally this would cause mild thoughts of tying her to the chair and burning the house down, but the last week has granted me an unparalleled level of calm.

"Jerald, I remember him. He was in my sociology class."

He was actually in her English composition class but there's no reason to tell her that.

"It doesn't say much, just that his family hasn't heard from him in a while and has reported him missing. 'Anyone with any information is encouraged to contact the police...'" She frowns, folding her paper up. We're sitting at her too-small breakfast counter, pantomiming a married couple.

And I don't mind.

She mentions a yard sale walk, some event at the college, and it is so easy to smile and nod. I feel a kinship with her in this moment; we were talking about a dead man a moment ago, and now we have easily moved on to a zombie movie screening put on by the film club.

Jerri begged for his life in a high-pitched voice, but sure babe, we can go get tacos after the yard sales. Yeah, I'd love to go out with you and your friends for your birthday next month. By the way, Jerri's blood was stickier than I thought it would be, like old fruit juice that's started to congeal.

We split off—she headed to work and I to class. A youthful, new-age Ozzie and Harriet. We are paragons of making it work. We are well-adapted young adults, tailor-made for a future filled to the brim with modern, suburbanite crispness. Our life will be aesthetic. Filtered. Any rough edges will be sliced off. We'll look so good in photos people will hate us but not be able to pinpoint exactly why. We will be sociopaths of the finest kind; monsters of living well. Living better than you.

There's a chunk of Jerri's jawbone in my pocket, polished clean. I run my thumb along the ridges, marveling at how I'd yanked and twisted it out.

God, I feel good.

I'm walking across campus, wondering what to have for lunch, when I spot the girl from Target making furious strides toward me. She cuts across the sidewalk, nearly knocking over a group of art students holding a bunch of posters until she is parallel with me, keeping stride. I smile at her. She's wearing yellow flannel and hideous purple jeans, but she looks good, smelling like some sort of licorice perfume.

"I know you," I say cheerfully.

"I saw what you did," she says in a tight, firm voice, low enough that only I can hear.

We cut across the large sweeping lawn toward the north building, our feet crushing leaves underneath us.

"What did I do?"

"I saw you at the Halloween party," she accuses. "With Jerri."

My hands are in my pockets, and I squeeze the jawbone. If there's a flicker of panic in my eyes, Cora doesn't see it.

"Oh, was he at that party?" I ask. "I didn't notice. I was with Natalie, so—"

We reach the door and I open it for her. Now we're in the stairwell, slowly climbing upwards. My class is on the second floor. I wonder if Cora the super-sleuth is going to follow me the whole time.

"You came back," she says. "You left the party with her. Then you came back and took Jerri."

I glance quickly at her. She doesn't speak with the standard hesitations and hitches that normal people do. There's no stutter, no intonations or... well, any emotion.

Interesting.

I stop on the landing of the second floor, and she freezes in front of me, not letting me get by her to the door.

"Where is he?" she demands. We're now face to face, and I can't help looking at her lips. There's a small scar on the bottom lip that the lipstick doesn't quite cover entirely. I wonder how it would feel pressed against my skin.

"I don't know," I reply. "I don't know what you believe you saw, but you're mistaken."

I try to brush past her, but she plants a hand on my chest. I smirk, and start to shove her away when a small, glittering knife appears out of nowhere and is suddenly pressed to my throat, digging in just under my Adam's apple. She pushes me against the wall, our backpacks thumping to the ground in a heap.

The door opens and the same group of students with their posters barge in, laughing with each other.

Cora lowers the knife slightly and presses her body against mine. Suddenly her lips are on my neck, kissing me just under the jaw, managing to block the knife from view. The art students grin at us and giggle before they disappear up the stairs.

She turns her head slightly to see if they're gone, and that's when I grab her wrist. Easily knocking the knife away, I spin her around and force her face first against the wall. Placing my hand on the back of her head, I press her cheek against the building roughly. Her arms flail helplessly until I gather them up and pin them behind her back.

"Let go of me, asshole," she growls.

"Nope."

We're both panting, and I have a feeling similar to when I was hunting Jerri. An excitement. This is *fun*. Finally, there are stakes, there's a threat, and there's something to defeat. An opponent.

Someone to play with.

I press against her and bring my lip to her ear. She's trembling with fury, and I almost laugh, but I manage to bring malice into my voice.

"Did you rehearse this? Did you say your little lines to your mirror before confronting the big bad man?" I lean down and grab the knife off the floor. It's a tiny little hunting knife with a porcelain doe carved into the handle. "Was your plan to threaten me with your adorable little knife and get me to *confess*?"

"Fuck. You," she hisses. "He hasn't answered his phone. Hasn't been at school, and he's not at his apartment. You killed him. I know you did."

I drop the knife over her shoulder, at her feet. I take the jawbone out of my pocket. I use it to brush the hair away from her cheek, and then caress her skin with it. Even though she doesn't get a good look at it, it gives me pleasure.

"You have no proof," I murmur in her ear. "Natalie will say I was with her all night. The houseguests will confirm it. The police won't be able to get a warrant."

"Fuck you!"

I grip her even tighter as she struggles to break free. Feeling the way she bucks against me leaves me almost breathless and I lean closer, my lips beside her ear. "And I'll be free to do whatever I want."

She stumbles as I finally release my hold on her, moving to grab my discarded bag and hoist it over my shoulder.

Cora turns around and glares at me. "I'm going to kill you," she bites out.

Twirling the jawbone fragment in my hand, I grin at her. "So, I guess I'll be seeing you around then, huh?"

Chapter Ten
Cora

I spend the next few days thinking about my encounter in the staircase with Target Guy. No matter what I do, I'm unable to get him out of my head. All my calls to Jerri go straight to voicemail. None of my texts have been delivered. To the world, he just vanished, and nobody even seems to have noticed his disappearance.

But I know he hasn't just run off. Ever since I've met him, he's always been dedicated to school. He would never leave without telling anyone. Especially me.

Jerri is dead. I just know it, and my encounter with Target Guy proves me right.

"I hate him," I tell my therapist, staring at the wall with vacant eyes.

"What is it that you dislike about this person?"

"Everything," I spit out, tapping my knee with my fingertips. "He thinks he can just do anything he wants without any consequences."

"Is that so?" he questions. "Did he tell you this?"

"I'm going to stop him."

He clears his throat and shifts in his chair. "How do you plan on stopping him?"

By slitting his throat—

"Cora?"

"I—I'm not sure," I stammer, sharply exhaling as I pinch the bridge of my nose between my fingers, trying to decipher my racing thoughts. "Ever since the day I met him, he's been in my head constantly. No matter how hard I try, I can't seem to make him go away—"

"That doesn't sound like dislike," he points out.

"He took my friend away from me," I rush out, shooting him a blank stare. "My only friend. He stole him from me. He cannot get away with this."

"When did this incident occur?"

I frown, avoiding his gaze. "Halloween night."

"And how did he 'take your friend away from you'?" he asks, clasping his hands together over his knee.

Well, he shoved him into the trunk of his car.

"Maybe your friend wasn't a real friend to begin with," he adds in.

"Oh, he had no choice in the matter. Trust me."

"Let's dig into that a little deeper," he says, his eyes exploring mine eagerly. "He had no choice?"

"No. He didn't."

"Everyone has a choice, Cora."

"You don't understand," I argue, my aggravation clear. "His choice was taken from him."

"How so?"

Letting out a sharp breath, I shake my head, searching for the right words.

"For fuck's sake," I snarl impatiently. "It just was."

"You're upset," he observes.

Finally, I glare at him. "No shit. You need a degree to make this obvious observation?"

"Have you talked to this other person?"

"Target Guy?" I ask, not even wanting to say his name. *Fuck you, Nolan.*

"Yes. Him. Perhaps you should tell him how you feel," he suggests.

Or perhaps I should bury my knife between his shoulder blades while I watch as he cries out in agony and sheer desperation.

"Perhaps," I say with a sadistic grin.

"Do you have feelings for this person, Cora?" he asks, catching me off guard. I blink at him, intermingled emotions of annoyance and disgust bubbling in my mind. "For either of them? Both?"

"That's not possible," I grit out, grinding my teeth. "I don't have feelings for anyone. I hate everyone equally. Jerri was the exception."

"And why is that?"

"Because he was my friend."

"No. You said you don't have feelings for anyone. That you hate everyone equally."

"Jerri never fucking bothered me like most people do," I snarl. "He never asked me stupid fucking questions, never once tried to change me, and he gave me space—"

"Why do you not allow yourself to have feelings for people, Cora?"

"Because they are useless. What's the point of having them, anyway?"

"Experiencing feelings in their entirety is a normal part of life."

"Well, I am *not* normal," I shoot back, watching him closely as he stands. He makes his way to where I'm positioned beside the window and stares into my eyes. "I'm the opposite of normal. You should know this." Rolling my eyes, I groan. "God, Michael. You really suck at your job. I hope you know that."

He chuckles, seeming to take it as if I were joking.

I shake my head at him. "Have you ever considered doing something else with your life? Something you're actually good at?"

"For someone who doesn't have feelings for anyone, you seem pretty upset about Jerri."

I'm upset because Target Guy gets to stroll around doing whatever his sadistic little heart desires while I'm stuck here with this moron.

Shrugging, I gaze out the window once more, looking down at the people walking on the sidewalks beside the busy roads. They're just living their lives, as if any of what they're doing in their day to day has meaning. How pathetic. They look like ants.

I want to squish them.

Putting them out of their misery would be the nice thing to do.

"Cora?"

"What?"

"I think the more important question here is, are you content with where you are now, in life, or do you want to change?"

"Change," I echo, folding my arms across my chest. "I don't know anymore. Even if I did, I don't know if I'm even capable of it—"

"You are," he speaks over me, tucking a loose strand of hair behind my ear. I freeze in place. He's looked at me like this before, like there's a fire burning within his eyes, but he's never actually touched me. Never acted on his impulses physically. "You are capable of anything, Cora. You just have to *want* it."

Catching his wrist with my hand, I squeeze it as hard as I can, holding it beside my head for a moment longer before swatting him away.

Confusion floods through me.

"Your support system is gone," he taunts, stepping closer. I immediately step back. "Your only friend is gone."

"I'm well aware," I mutter.

He plants a firm hand on my shoulder. "You must feel alone right now," he points out, wetting his lips with the tip of his tongue. "*Very* alone."

"Do I?" My voice is a challenge, and my face is blank. I blink up at him, waiting for his reply.

"Yes." He slips his arms around my waist without warning and takes my ass in his hands, giving my flesh a firm squeeze.

"But you have me," he announces, finally revealing his true self. His true intentions. "I'm here for you, Cora."

My body immediately reacts to his suggestive touch. I recoil, taking several steps back while he studies my reaction.

"I fucking knew it," I declare.

He says nothing, although the expression on his face almost appears disappointed with my rejection, as if I had failed his test.

Yes.

That is exactly what this advance on me was.

A test.

My hands ball into fists at my sides as I get the sudden urge to castrate him. Instead of acting on this impulse, I find myself turning away and heading for the door.

"Cora," he calls out from behind me. "I'm only trying to help you. You do understand that don't you?"

Glancing over my shoulder hastily, I glare at him. "Don't bother trying to explain yourself. You're just worried I'm going to run to mommy or the cops and tell them how my creepy doctor crossed the line and groped my ass."

He blinks at me, mouth agape, unsure as to what he could possibly say to make me stay.

"Well, I'm not," I tell him. "And for what it's worth, even if I did tell them, they wouldn't believe me anyway. Nobody ever does."

With that, I slam the door behind me.

Chapter Eleven

Nolan

"You seem distant lately," Natalie points out. The statement comes veering in from a faraway galaxy, an entirely different species of life form uttering it from her mouth.

I'm walking along a breezy downtown district with a foamy, too-sweet coffee in my hand and Natalie is staring at me curiously. I hear sirens in the far distance and while I realize they're not for me, the thought occurs anyway.

What if they are?

Does it kick off as a frantic scramble, a bloody chase, a screaming end in bloodshed and chaos?

I smile at Natalie and wonder if it'd be a good idea to take her hostage. "I've been feeling a little... blah, you know?"

We walk past a boutique, and I can smell a sweet aroma wafting from the gourmet cupcake shop down the block. Natalie is fidgeting as she walks, touching her face too much and twirling her hair in that way that tells me she's struggling to say something.

I zone out; Cora is drifting back into my daydream. Suddenly, I'm not taking Natalie hostage. No. Instead, Cora and I are speeding away from flashing police lights together with a body in the trunk and oceans of blood in our future.

"I feel like you're not that interested in me," Natalie from another galaxy says.

I look at her and know how easy this would be to fix. I could take her hand right now and tell her that I cherish her but I'm simply going through something right now. An identity crisis perhaps, devolving into a series of questions around what I want to do with my life, who I want to be, the usual nonsense people tell each other. Perhaps here might even be a ring of truth to it. Enough to make it resonate with her.

Or I could manipulate her into thinking it was her fault. Tell her that the relationship is one-sided and that I'm the only one working to please her. I'll even add on that she hasn't shown much interest in me beyond making me a fuckable accessory to her life. I could catch her accusation and hurl it back with such firmness that her lack of confidence would cause her to blame herself. Her own doubt would work against her, undermining objective truth.

"You did it again." Natalie is snapping her fingers in my face. "You get that flat look in your eyes, and you're just *gone.*"

"What are you talking about?"

"I told you something was bothering me and it's like you don't even care," she complains.

I lean away from her fingers and open my mouth to deliver something to keep the relationship going. This is a small scratch on the surface of us and I can fix it with a bandage of words.

"I really don't like you. You feel like an insect to me. Like a ladybug that has landed on my shirt. It was nice for a while... the ladybug. But now?" I shrug. "It's time to flick you off."

The wrong words leave me, but I watch them with a particular savage glee. The look on her face is of shock and hurt, and if I don't leave soon there will be tears. I hand her my coffee cup—I'm not entirely sure why I hand it to her or why she takes it—and walk away. I hear her speak, once, but I'm walking too fast to make it out clearly.

It sounds like "Are you kidding me?" which makes me break into a wide smile.

The game with Cora can finally have my full attention.

Nolan

I spend the next few days in a state of mild alert, waiting for Cora to lunge out of various bushes and alleyways, checking my rearview mirror for a car that follows me for too long. I check over my shoulder as I walk around campus and wait for stern-faced detectives to appear and ask if I "have a moment for a few questions."

Nothing happens. No black-haired girl tries to stab me, no police raids, nothing.

I'm almost disappointed.

I have to lay low for a while before picking out my next victim. They haven't found the remains of Jerri yet and I doubt they will.

But two disappearances in a mid-sized town will start to bring attention.

Though, I don't want to settle into date nights with Natalie, turning in essays on Mondays, and going to work on Tuesdays while waiting to be myself again.

One day, after class, I ignore Natalie's third call of the day and instead head to the store. I tell myself it's to get trash bags, zip ties, and tools for the next kill—the first one was so, so messy—and totally, definitely not to see if Cora is working.

It's the first time anyone has known what I am.

My parents are cookie-cutter suburbanites with jobs in offices. They are business-casual amalgamations, sweater vests and khakis. They aren't capable of any sort of violence, of any sort of change. They are less than people; just shadows flitting from one task to the next.

Sometimes I daydream about dragging a body—hacked up and full of my teeth marks—and dropping it into the middle of the living room. What would they do? I don't think they would react. My mother might look up briefly from her crossword and ask me not to track dirt on her rug.

My father might sigh and ask if I had decided on a career yet.

I might spiral into a cackling murder spree, be dragged off and thrown into a state dungeon for crimes too heinous to mention, but at the end of the day, I don't think I'm any more of a sociopath than my parents.

I find myself standing in a long checkout line, holding a random assortment of objects I grabbed as I wandered the aisles. Ahead of me, I can see Cora bitterly scanning items. She hasn't seen me yet.

I'm holding a pair of socks, two candle lighters, and a can of tomato soup.

The line inches forward and she glances up and sees me, her eyes narrowing slightly as she offers no other reaction.

I watch her fake smile at the other customers, enjoying the very act of looking at her. There is a sharp angularity to her features that attract me to her, with her almost gray eyes made darker by the black mascara. Her hair is in a ponytail today and I notice small, silver hoop earrings dangling from her ears.

I wonder how they would taste; the metal mixed with the softness of her earlobes, taking them gently in my mouth.

My phone vibrates and I'm brutally reminded of Natalie, who messages and asks if we can talk later.

I sigh.

I'm next in line, just behind a middle-aged man buying an armload of paper towels, paper plates, and paper cups. I catch her shooting furious glances at me as she haphazardly scans the items and throws them into bags. She glares at me while the man fumbles with his debit card and pays for his stuff, and then I slide up, placing my items on the belt.

"Hi," I say.

"Why are you here?" she asks blankly, scanning the lighter.

I pause with a frown, then opt to tell the truth. "I wanted to see you."

The words hit her, and she looks down for a moment as if baffled. "What, you want to talk? Is that it?"

"I guess."

She scowls. "Why?"

I lean in, staring her straight in the eyes. "We share a secret, and this is much more interesting than anything else I have going on."

She scans the rest of my items, a carefully passive look on her face. Finally, as she's handing me the receipt, she says, "I get off in ten minutes."

The sun is sinking rapidly in the sky, a hazy orange orb that seems desperate to leave the horizon. I'm leaning against my car as Cora comes out, her body language defensive. And I notice that she's clutching her keys in her fist looking ready to fight.

"I'm not going to murder you," I say.

"Sure. No one has *ever* said that and then stabbed someone." She stops in front of me, standing only mere inches away. "So, what is this?" Her hands motion between our chests. "What's the point of this? You gonna kill me next?"

I lean easily back on my car. "I can't kill you even if I wanted to. Two people from the same party go missing? Every part-time detective, true crime podcast and Facebook group will be looking for a suspect. Plus, a pretty girl goes missing, well, people notice."

Her arms cross and she flips her hair off her shoulder.

"You want to get to the fucking point?" she spits.

I hesitate. I didn't think this through. I don't have much of a plan more of a simple, direct... *feeling*. I'm not sure how to handle it. I just want to see her. My brain offers a variety of ways to try and manipulate her, lure her into traps, but I reject them all. I don't know what I want. I just revisit the way she looked at the knives that night.

So, I choose truth.

Standing in the pockmarked, potholed parking lot of a Target with the only person who knows I'm a murderer, I choose truth.

"I think you're just like me," I say to her, carefully watching how she reacts.

"Oh, yeah?" It's a challenge. She hasn't run off. She isn't fumbling for her phone to call the police. She is meeting my eyes and daring me to keep talking.

"Yes. I think there's something a little off about you. You hide it well—" I circle behind her, my chest brushing against her shoulder, "and you drift through life, but nothing feels real. Like it has any stakes."

I brush a loose strand of hair off her arm, still circling until I'm in front of her, face to face.

"You killed my friend," she states. "My *only* friend."

"I did. And I enjoyed it. And I'm going to do it again... and again... and again..."

I lower my voice with each syllable, the jovial face of Nolan dropping and my true face appearing. Her eyes flick to my lips, and her façade begins to crack.

"Who do you think you are, *Nolan*?" she says, and I feel a wild thrill at my name leaving her mouth. "You think you're this dangerous, cold monster?" Her hand comes up and jabs me in the chest. "You're just a murderer. That's it. There's nothing special about you."

I laugh, turn away and get in my car. She's standing there, incredulous. I start it up and roll down the window, sticking my head out.

"You talk tough," I taunt, "but we both know you're getting in my car."

There's anger on her face—there's always anger on her face, Jesus Christ—but her mouth twitches, teasing at a smile. She stomps over and gets in, and for the first time in my life, I have a passenger for one of my night drives.

Chapter Twelve

Cora

We race down darkened roads, the headlights barely keeping up with us, taking curves at speed, the tires kissing the dirt shoulder as we leave the glow of fast-food restaurants and gas stations entering never-ending darkness. Trees and tangled woods press on all sides as the houses get fewer and fewer in between. It feels like we're escaping, civilization melting into the background.

He says nothing. He just drives, one wrist draped loosely over the steering wheel. He glances at me every so often, until eventually he breaks the silence.

"What does it feel like for you?"

I play dumb, because letting him in would be a big mistake. I already know this doesn't end well.

"What do you mean?" I ask.

He taps the center of his forehead. "For me, everything feels like paper. *Thin.* Like I can punch through it. It's not that nothing matters, it's that everything feels loose and inconsequential. Nothing attaches, really. I have to pretend, go through the motions and construct this image of a functioning person."

There's a knife in my boot. I can feel it against my ankle every time the car jostles. For the last few days, I've been obsessing over all the different ways I could kill him. Ways I could find the same high I had gotten when I chased that Tinder guy around my apartment with my knife. Now, I have the perfect opportunity. I'm going to stab him and leave him in the woods, take his car and disappear.

I'm gripping the armrest, waiting for him to say more. There's a strange feeling twisting in my chest, something beyond the normal rage that bubbles there. I struggle to comprehend what I'm hearing. There's a sense of relief in knowing that someone else is caught in this chaotic in-between of knowing you're disconnected and a borderline psychopath, but also being aware enough that you are not normal. That you are an aberration. That an entire society is built around these ideas of attachment and empathy that you simply do not possess.

Michael has tried to convince me that I can change, that it's not okay for me to feel this way. That I'm all alone in this world and that nobody else would ever understand.

It's another animal entirely hearing it come out of the mouth of someone else, another human gliding through life like it's a boring dream and they're just waiting for it to be over.

My therapist really fucking sucks at his job.

"What about your girlfriend?" I question, already knowing the answer. If Nolan is anything like me, I know the answer.

"She's like a plant," Nolan replies, shrugging. "Or a pet. I think people like pets more, but—"

My mind flickers to when I was a kid, looking down at the dead family dog, wondering how I was supposed to react.

"She's not my girlfriend, by the way," he tells me. "We broke up."

My eyes widen with amusement. "How did that happen?"

He shifts in his seat, appearing to consider it. "I thought that I wanted to camouflage a part of myself. Hide in this idea of a loving relationship, a stable life. But the more I dig into it the more I want to tear it apart." He pauses. "It's like I'm hungry, and I keep eating, but nothing satisfies the hunger."

Nolan is waiting for me to respond. He has offered up a piece of himself and wants to see if I will echo the vulnerability. Everything is a test. Everything is leverage. I try to talk, but the words are tough to get out.

"I've never killed anyone," I tell him. "I want to. It's all I think about lately. Sometimes I think about hurting people and they're the clearest, purest thoughts I have." I become silent for a moment, unsure of how to continue. "Most of all, though... I've always wondered how it would feel to be in someone's skin."

He presses down on the accelerator, and we go a little faster. His sharp jaw is clenched for a long time and when he finally speaks, I can tell he's disguising his thoughts in a joke, wrapping a feeling he doesn't understand into something that can be dismissed.

"Cora," he says, grinning slightly, "we might be mutual monsters."

CAUTION TAPE

Nolan

We hit a deer on the way back. It's too perfect. It darts into the road, gives us a startled look, then tries to bolt, but the front bumper clips it as we race past, a dull *thud* echoing in the car.

Cora doesn't flinch.

I ease the car to the shoulder of the road and shut it off.

"Glovebox," I tell Cora. "There's a flashlight, a knife, and gloves."

"Do it yourself."

I retrieve the flashlight and gloves, watching her closely as her gaze sets on the knife. "Go on," I instruct.

Without any further hesitation, she grabs hold of it, looking at me from the corner of her eye. I shouldn't trust her with the knife. I also shouldn't walk in front of her, but I do anyway, enjoying the thrill and half-anticipating to feel the sting of the blade in my back. She follows me into the woods past the tree line and even deeper toward the direction I saw the deer fleeing in.

The flashlight manages to find a loose trail of broken vegetation the animal crashed through, pushing bushes and brambles out of the way in its panic. There's a small, trickling blood trail I keep the light trained on.

"What are we doing?"

"The deer we hit is hurt," I tell her. "This is something I do when it gets to be too much, and I need to unleash it. Find an animal and kill it."

She's walking beside me now, our feet crushing sticks and twigs, the small orb from the flashlight bouncing in front of us.

"Does it help?" she asks.

Our shoulders touch briefly as we crest a small hill. "It quiets things down for a little while."

The deer is laying limply in a small clearing, leaning against a splintered, fallen tree-trunk. When it sees us, it struggles to try and stand, but the back-half of its body sags and it collapses again.

Cora beats me to it, looming over it. I hand her the gloves. I put one foot on the quivering deer, holding it down while she slides them on, a serene expression on her face. She tosses the knife from hand to hand.

I laugh. "Quit stalling. Unless you're all talk." I shine the flashlight in her face, making her blink. "Or you could just go back to your boring little life. Go back to being a rude little bitch with a dead friend. Or—" I shine the light down at the deer, "we can play in blood together."

She sinks to her knees, and I can't help but picture her doing that for me. Looking up at me she tilts her chin.

"Fuck you, Nolan."

The knife glints dangerously in the dim pulse of the flashlight before being driven into the stomach of the deer with a frenzy that shocks me. Cora's face is twisted almost beyond recognition as the deer bucks and shrieks, twisting underneath my foot. One of its hooves kick out and grazes her lip, drawing blood, but it doesn't faze her.

She grabs the leg, pinning it down and digging the knife back into the abdomen of the animal. She's not trying to kill it. She's trying to make it suffer. She hits something major with the blade and a gout of blood spurts out, coating her arms, neck, and chest. It turns her from a forgettable suburban woman in the woods into a demonic shadow, flickering in the low beam of the flashlight, coated in crimson. The blood doesn't stop her. I don't think I could stop her either.

The deer goes completely still, yet she's still hacking away at it, carving a hole into the side of the creature. Its entrails spill out and slide onto the ground in a mess of dirt and gore.

"Cora," I say, and she slows down, panting heavily while looking up at me, her visage covered in the result of her own violence.

"That was..." She gulps air, stretching her fingers and arms eyes shining with amazement at what she's done. A smile claims her face as I help her to her feet. "It was just that... *finally*. I could *finally* let go."

"I know."

She is still breathing hard, chest heaving, but I see it coming. I feel the air change. And the way that she readjusts the grip on the knife, looking down to throw me off. The flashlight is starting to die, and the woods have darkened completely. An enveloping blackness pressing against us.

A twig breaks as she shifts her weight and swings the knife in a driving arc, trying to bury it in the center of my chest.

Silly little bitch.

Her arms are tired so she's slow. Too slow. She has to know that. I turn sideways and she lunges past me, easily allowing me to catch her wrist and bend it, making her cry out. As a result, she drops the knife. Pulling her arm as hard as I can, I yank her to me like a doll. Gathering both her arms and pinning them behind her back, I force her body against mine. She looks up at me, face contorted in a grimace. She smells like blood and sweat. Her hair is matted and tangled. She feels wet and warm against me.

"Still trying to kill me?" I rasp.

"I told you I would," she replies softly.

I yank her damp shirt over her head, my hands tacky and sticky with blood. Her skin feels soft and hot as I peel her flimsy bra off and take one of her nipples in my mouth, biting down on it gently but firmly enough that I feel her nails dig into the back of my head.

I pull back and take off my shirt. The moment it's discarded she gleefully runs her hands down my chest, and I can feel a long streak of blood left behind. Unbuckling my belt, she tugs it out of the loops with a wry smile, and that's when it clicks; she's always been in control.

"Did I say you could do that?" I taunt, swatting her hands away.

It's dark, the flashlight is on the ground barely giving us enough light to see each other, but her eyes are wide and incredulous.

"What?" she asks.

I grab her by the chin, lifting her up onto her tiptoes so that she has to shakily take a step toward me. My other hand gathers her hair up, twisting it slightly so that she gasps in pain.

"Open your mouth," I demand, yanking her head back.

She presses her lips in a firm, straight line, glaring at me.

Laughing, I snake my hand down and unbutton her stupid little work khakis, watching her squirm as I unzip them before tugging them along her curved hips.

"Open your *fucking* mouth," I say again, but all she does is raise her eyebrows.

Cora, Cora, Cora.

My palm trails down her stomach and I slip my hand over her panties, my hand too big to fit fully, my knuckles scraping against the zipper of the khaki's. I can only move three of my fingers, but the moment I touch her I hear her inhale sharply through her nose. She bucks her hips as I slowly stroke her clit, moving my fingers against her in firm rotations, the zipper digging into my skin as I work her faster.

Her knees buckle and a moan escapes her, but she manages to keep her mouth closed. I remove my hand, and she lets out a frustrated groan.

"If you want to come... you're going to open your mouth."

Still, she's defiant. I like that. I hook my fingers around the belt loop of her pants and tug them down until they fall around her knees. I stretch the waistband of her panties and let it snap back against her hip.

"Take these off," I order.

It's something I could easily do, but I want to make her do it. It's turning me on to have her defiant yet playing along, this push-and-pull making everything that much more delicious.

Cora locks eyes with me and pulls them down. Then, still gazing at me, opens her mouth, letting her tongue hang out.

Fuck.

I stick two of my fingers in her mouth and she bites down, hard. Then she grins and starts to slowly work her tongue along the digits, tickling and sucking them. She lets go, and I immediately bury my hand between her thighs, tracing her clit with my fingers, rubbing her with delicious friction.

"Yes," she whimpers.

"Yeah?" I taunt, thrusting two fingers inside her as she clings to me, desperately trying to hold herself upright.

"Oh, fuck!" she cries out suddenly, groaning with pleasure, her body collapsing against me.

"Really? I haven't even started," I mutter in her ear.

With one swift motion I toss her onto the ground. She lands hard, staring up at me with fresh anger while I tear off her pants and shoes in a hurried frenzy. Pulling my cock out of my pants, I crawl onto her, gripping her shoulder hard. Fingers digging into her skin while I move my hips and position myself along her slit, the head dipping along her clit just enough to make her draw in a breath. Before she can let it out again, I thrust inside of her forcefully, feeling her warmth as her walls tighten.

"It hurts," she spits out, eyes wide, mouth agape. "It hurts so good. Holy fuck—"

"There's nothing holy about the way I plan on fucking you," I warn, hooking my arm around her thigh while my other hand grips her throat.

Her fingernails dig into my back as I slam into her as deep as her body allows. Building up speed until I'm pounding into her, I raise myself up for leverage, locking eyes with her as she glares at me.

"Go to hell, Nolan," she utters, her voice rising with mine in mutual, agonizing pleasure.

With that, I slam into her deeper; harder. Again and again, working my hips in steady, aggravated rhythms.

"I'm gonna turn you over and fuck you from behind, right here in the dirt," I warn her, flipping her onto her stomach before burying myself inside her once more.

"Harder!" she cries out with each stroke, her screams echoing through the emptiness of the surrounding woods.

That's when I lose all composure, fucking her as hard as I can. My pelvis collides harshly with her round ass and our skin smacks loudly. With my knees digging into the ground, I tighten my grasp on her hips and drive into her savagely.

"Yes!" she screams, pushing back and meeting my every thrust. Her body tenses as I lean against her, locking my fingers around her throat and cutting off her air supply.

"I'm—" she chokes out, convulsing against me. "Oh, God, I'm going to—"

"Damn right you are."

Monsters, indeed.

Chapter Thirteen

Nolan

Nothing is said as we get our clothes back on and walk back to the car. The engine clicks on, the lights snap to life, and we drive away. I catch glimpses of us in the reflection of the mirrors and windows. Our hair is tangled, with leaves and grass caught in it, faces smeared with blood and dirt. There is a twig in my shoe. We look like we crawled out of graves.

I pull up to her car that we left in the store parking lot, catching my reflection in the rearview mirror to realize that we look even worse under the harsh lights of civilization.

"This changes nothing," Cora says.

"Okay."

"Nothing," she reiterates.

She gets out, slamming the door without looking back. Smiling to myself, I drive away.

Why would I want things to change?

Cora

It's been years since I've last smoked a cigarette, but after my encounter with Nolan out in the woods, I'm dying for the harsh burn of a nicotine fix. Opening the window in my bedroom, I spark one up, inhaling a much needed drag.

I breathe out a thick cloud of smoke, sinking onto the floor with my back pressed to the wall. Squeezing my eyes shut, I replay the memories from earlier.

Killing the deer.

The sight of blood, and the enticing glow of the red liquid was almost just enough to send me to an orgasm. The intoxicating scent of copper overwhelmed my senses and left me falling into a bottomless well of euphoria.

Adrenaline.

That surely must have been what sent me over the brink.

Right?

Tossing back another shot of vodka, I cringe, trying to shake away unwanted thoughts. Although, it fails to work.

Instead, I see Nolan, covered in sweat and blood, the muscles flexing in his arms and shoulders as he fucked me into the dirt.

The way he felt spread like cool vines in my mind. Seeding thoughts of the way he made me feel. Blossoming into the keening cries of the way he made me come.

"Jesus Christ," I mutter to myself, putting my cigarette out on the windowsill before climbing into bed.

No man has ever been able to get me off. Not until tonight. Not until *Nolan*.

It had to have been a fluke. I was concentrating on what I had done to the deer just moments before. The thrill of my first kill is what truly did it.

Right?

Shit.

There's only one way to find out for sure.

"Cora," Michael says as I stroll into his office unannounced. He glances up at the wall of clocks before his eyes return to mine. "I wasn't expecting you."

"The other day," I begin, locking the door behind me. "You said you were here for me." I pause, making my way to his desk.

His eyes narrow as he watches me.

"Are you?" I ask with a grimace. "Are you really '*here for me*?"

Before anything else can leave my mouth, he crosses the room with predatory ease, spinning me around and managing to bend me over his desk. There it is. The mask has fallen away, and I can see him for what he truly is.

At the end of the day, he just wants something from me. If he really cared about my wellbeing, even the slightest bit, then he wouldn't be yanking up my skirt the way he is now. He wouldn't be groping my ass, and he most certainly wouldn't be slipping his hand between my thighs.

Little does he know... I want something from him, too.

Gripping the edge of the desk, I suck my lower lip into my mouth. His fingertips lightly brush the skin over my hips as he eases my underwear down my legs, caressing my skin with ice cold fingers. I lift my foot and step out of them. Michael kicks my ankle to the side with the tip of his shoe, spreading my legs wider before easing a finger inside of me.

I flinch.

He's really wasting no time.

"You feel exactly how I've imagined, Cora," he breathes heavily, thrusting his long, lean finger into me over and over again. My inner walls grip him tightly as I push back against his hand, taking him deeper. "Tight. Wet." He lets out a soft moan while lowering himself and takes the flesh of my ass into his mouth, biting down gently. "So very wet for me."

I remain silent, gripping the edge of his desk tighter as he begins to finger fuck me. He grunts sharply with each thrust forward.

I shut my eyes, allowing myself to drift away, engulfed with the most intense sensations. I know this is considered wrong. Look at us, doctor and patient. The abuse of power sends me spiraling, wetness dripping from my pussy and coating my thighs.

Michael removes his hand from between my legs. "Hold on to the desk, Cora," he instructs as he yanks down his pants. He slams his cock all the way inside of me without wasting another second. God, he is massive. Almost as big as Nolan.

He pulls out quickly only to thrust into me harder. In. Out. In, and back out.

The sporadic thrusting of his hips doesn't fit into a rhythm and it's clear that he's only looking for his own end here.

I suck my bottom lip into my mouth once more, holding back hisses and moans. Fuck, it actually hurts. The desk rocks violently as he pounds into me, his fingernails digging into my hips. The taste of copper overwhelms my senses. I've bitten my lip too hard, drawing blood.

Blood… blood… blood.

Gutting the deer crosses my mind.

He has drawn blood, too. I can feel the harsh stinging of the small slits in my skin. I hate long fingernails on men. He should really get them trimmed. Michael quickens his pace, smacking his hips against my ass as he takes exactly what he wants.

Me.

"Jesus Christ," I snarl.

He pays me no mind, slamming into me more forcefully without giving even the slightest of fucks.

"Tell me how this feels," he orders in a smooth tone. "How does my big, meaty cock feel when it's buried inside of you?"

The small jar of pens to the side of me falls over. They roll off the desk and clatter against the floor, straying in all different directions. The computer wobbles back and forth and all of his paperwork scatters.

"It's fine."

A dull ache settles between my thighs from the sheer force he's using. He fucks like a wild animal who has gone rabid.

"Fine?" he growls. "Just fine?"

"Well, is that all you've got?" I breathe out, craning my neck to look back at him. "Fuck me harder."

Suddenly, he tangles his fingers in my hair and forces my cheek down against the cool, hard surface of his mahogany desk, ensuring that I'm unable to move. Each gasp of air he draws in is shorter and more desperate than the last. I clench my jaw, stifling whimpers and all signs of discomfort as he grants my wish.

"Cora," he cries out, slamming into me aggressively. "Oh, *Cora*."

With one long stroke, he empties himself inside of me, leaving me completely unsatisfied.

Worthless as ever.

Just another *worthless, useless man.*

Struggling to gain control of his breathing, he remains deep inside of me for the next minute or so until his cock becomes soft. I don't say a single word. I have none to offer.

I yawn instead.

He strolls around his desk and into my view, tucking his dick back into his pants and fastening his belt. "How was that, Cora?" he asks.

I hold back an unimpressed laugh. He's big. I'll give him that. In the end, I was left bored, the easy realization that he wasn't Nolan now staring me in the face.

"From this point further, I believe twice weekly sessions would benefit you more," he tells me, smoothing out his long sleeve button up shirt. It is a tacky navy blue, I notice absently. "How does that sound?"

"Benefit me?" I ask, my voice trailing off. "Or you?"

His jaw clenches tight. "Both."

Without showing further interest in the conversation, I stand upright. "Sounds fine, Michael," I reply.

"Time is up."

Retrieving my panties from the floor, I use them to clean myself up, tossing them onto the desk without another word.

Nolan

I feel unleashed on the world for the first time in my existence. I was a drowning victim, choking on normalcy and the facsimile of a grinning face.

No longer.

There's so much to do before I begin my work in earnest. I need a place to take victims to toy with them. I need a way to dispose of their bodies. I need better gloves and better knives. I need routes of police patrols. I need binoculars to watch potential victims and get a sense of their routine. I can no longer simply hide amongst the student population. The town isn't big enough, anonymity is an evaporating resource.

I need to become organized and lethal, or the blood will be cut off before it can truly begin to flow. I will then simply be another smirking maniac in orange prison fatigues; instead of something truly irredeemable, truly horrific that causes shudders when the teeming hordes of soccer moms, baseball dads, accountants, PTA members, cashiers, lawyers, and all of the bleak, woefully mundane humans hear of what I've done to the creatures that could've been them. I want them to cover their mouths and shy away from their own potential wreckage.

What I shouldn't do is cruise around in my car, reliving moments with Cora. It's a flashing, strobe effect on my mind where for a moment I'm thinking of the knife sinking into Jerald. The satisfaction it gave me to lay him out flat and begin hitting his bones with a small hammer; shattering tibias, patellae, and all sorts of fun smaller pieces, all while seeing how the human body could be so...

Crunchy.

Then the strobe flashes, and my mind seizes on the image of Cora, drawing the form of her to me. It's the feeling of her against me; the warmth of her skin and the way that heart of hers went *thud-thud, thud-thud, thud-thud*, growing louder and faster the harder I fucked her in the dirt. My mind teemed with how her pulse seemed to throw itself against my hand when I gripped her neck and those vibrant eyes blazed with malice and lust.

I have a hundred things to do. A minefield of stalking, police evasion, and wonderful murder lay before me, and I needed to focus.

How would it feel to have her down on her knees for you, her hands tied behind her back, looking up at you...

I need plastic wrap. I need to find a location that is secluded and soundproof. I might need a different vehicle, too. I can't keep using my car for this. That's too obvious...

That scar that splits her bottom lip... I want to watch her trail it up the length of my cock, keeping her eyes on mine the entire time. I want to see that wicked smile as she says "Fuck you, Nolan" in that pouty voice, right before I grab the back of her head and make her gag on it.

Maybe shipping containers can wait. Maybe the treasure trove of homicidal toys I want can be pushed off until tomorrow.

I turn the car around in someone's driveway and speed off in the direction of Cora's job, hoping she'll be there.

I pass flowers on the way into the store—a rack of them—and resist the urge to grab a bouquet. I am swirling in a mixture of elation and confusion, second guessing every fleeting emotion that decides to rear its head, trying to fend them off with ruthless rationalization.

I'm only interested because she's a challenge.

Once she's dealt with, it'll be over, and my sense of balance will return. This is nothing more than a fun new game for my gnashing mind to grapple with. Nothing more.

I'm fuming in these thoughts as I carefully walk through the store, approaching the checkout counters on multiple passes, getting closer each time. I finally see her, sitting with her arms folded, glaring at a man dressed like a social worker who sits across from her.

I imagine breaking one of the fluorescent overhead lights, ripping out one of the long bulbs, breaking in two over my knee, and digging the serrated glass edge into this guy's neck. I would pull it firmly through the gristle of his throat, shredding the flesh and sending a torrent of dark, oxygen-starved blood all over the table.

The urge disappears as I approach them; Cora sees me over the man's shoulder and tenses. The man turns around and surveys me.

"Ah... hello. Would this be—*ahem*—Target Guy?" he asks Cora.

She nods, her eyes flicking between us as I reach out to shake his hand.

"Nolan. I'm a friend of Cora's."

He shakes my hand and sighs in a pedantic, lecture sort of way.

"Nolan, you seem well intentioned. I wonder if you understand that you're doing something... off-putting?" He glances at Cora, who tightens her lips but doesn't respond. "Anyway, as someone who's interested in her well-being, I—"

"Cora, who's the substitute teacher you're talking to?" I nod my head at him, and he sighs again.

"Michael. My therapist," she mutters. Michael reaches over the table and squeezes her arm in a reassuring manner.

Behind my eyes there is something wicked, dark, and drooling. It's desperate to claw its way out and sever every limb Michael has.

"A core part of her therapy is going to be teaching her to set boundaries with people in her life. Especially people who are bothering her."

I'm standing awkwardly over them, attracting glances as people walk by with their shopping bags. The conversation needs to end before I am "seen with the victim before his disappearance".

"This doesn't seem very professional. Do therapists normally talk to people for their patients?" I look at Cora. Here was a girl ready to stab me in the woods, and now she's acting like a scolded child because of... this guy?

"Well," Michael says, "Cora and I are approaching her treatment in an unorthodox way."

The knowing smile he gives Cora makes me want to cut off his ears and stuff them in his eye sockets.

"We have decided it would be best if you kept your distance," he continues. "I think you have some work to do on yourself and your relationship with Cora is just not healthy."

I am Nolan. I am in control. I have always been in control. I will not lose it here in this *fucking* Target.

Ignoring him, I address Cora. "If you ever want to be *not healthy...* text me." Her phone is sitting on the table in front of her, unlocked and inviting. I lean in and pluck it away, swiping to contacts and adding my number. I hand it back to her, my eyes catching hers. "I don't see anything wrong with you."

"That's enough." Michael is standing now, glaring at me. Cora quickly takes her phone back, and I saunter away, offering a few stray glances back at Michael as I go.

Chapter Fourteen

Nolan

They emerge from the store after quite some time. I maintain my watch from the camouflage of my own vehicle as they walk across the parking lot. They appear to be arguing; Cora is gesturing wildly with her hands. They get into a car—his car—and drive away. I start my own car up and begin following them, keeping at a distance, a few cars between us.

Cora has an idea of what I am, but Michael does not. I have that advantage.

I drum my hands on the steering wheel and lean around in my seat, craning my neck to keep track of Michael's silver sedan. I have a very loose, general sort of plan, and that bothers me. This is impulsive and I know it. All of this increases the likelihood of getting caught. More people and more variables. I am on the verge of my second kill, a seminal moment in my ascension.

Anyone can take a singular life. The next step of solidifying myself in routines and obsessions is very important to me. It deserves patience and attention, not a breathless, hasty murder because I am jealous of the guy with the pretty girl.

And that's all it is, right?

Just pure, normal jealousy.

All the musings on how horrific and distant I am from normal emotional responses and here I am—the jilted lover—stalking a girl and her boyfriend like any other modern loser.

I laugh loudly in my empty car and press down on the gas, bringing Michael's car further into view.

The thrill of stalking my prey combines with the joy of potential self-destruction. All of it for the sake of that dark-haired, gorgeous nightmare.

Cora

"What the fuck is your problem?" I snap, staring up at him with irritation as he shuts my door with a loud thud. He's upset. This is clear.

Though that's far from my problem.

Michael climbs into the driver's seat and releases a sharp breath, grasping the wheel hard enough that it causes his knuckles to shine white.

"You told me you didn't feel anything for him," he scolds.

I glare at him through narrowed eyes. "I don't," I shoot back.

"I saw the way you looked at him."

"What's it to you, anyway?"

"I am your *therapist*—"

"Exactly," I cut him off. "You're my therapist, not my fucking boyfriend. Learn your goddamn place."

I watch him closely as he starts up the engine and begins to drive recklessly through the parking lot, the car bouncing through every pothole.

"Let me out," I order. "I'm not even finished with my shift yet."

"We need to talk about this, Cora," he retorts, flashing me a brief, condescending stare. "We've talked about how you sleeping with random men is reckless behavior. You're simply trying to fill the void inside you."

"Oh, so sleeping with *you* is an exception, right?"

"I'm helping you," he mutters, taking a sharp turn out onto the main road.

"I didn't realize getting railed by my therapist who is at least fifteen years older than me is a form of therapy."

"Age doesn't matter."

"You're fucking married," I laugh, my gaze drifting to his wedding band. "You don't even bother trying to hide it. Does your wife know what you really do at work? That you spend your therapy sessions shoving your *meaty* cock inside of your patients?"

"Only you," he tries to clarify. "It's only you."

"That's what they all say," I murmur. "As if that somehow makes it acceptable."

"This is all a part of your treatment, Cora. This is different."

"How so?"

"We will discuss this further when we get to my office."

I blink at him, waiting for him to look over at me, but he doesn't. He continues to stare straight out the windshield with determination in his eyes. Shifting in my seat, I let out an annoyed breath, gazing out my window bleakly.

Sleeping with him was only supposed to be a test. A one-time thing.

Clearly, he's taking it to a whole new level.

When we pull up to a luxurious looking house in a nice neighborhood, I can't help but roll my eyes. The bastard lied to me. He's taken me to his house.

"You've got some balls," I groan. "I thought you said we were going to your office?"

"I also work from home."

"Whatever."

Right on cue, I pull out my phone and search for Nolan's name in my contacts. When I find him, I shoot him a quick text.

Me: I think I might want to be unhealthy.
Me: Scratch that. I want to be a lunatic.

"No," Michael lets out unexpectedly. "Do not text him. Give me your phone."

My eyes lock with his as he pulls into a driveway. "What?"

Without warning, he tears it from my grasp and exits the car.

A rush of adrenaline courses through me, the blood boiling in my veins. I fling my door open and practically leap out of the car, storming in his direction and chasing him all the way up to the front entrance.

"Give me my phone, jackass," I demand, done with his games.

He unlocks the front door and strolls inside. I follow behind him, now in a fit of rage.

"Give me my fucking phone," I say again, burying my hand into his pants pocket until he swats my arm away. Little white spots begin to cloud my vision, and my body vibrates with an anger so intense I find myself scanning the entryway for heavy objects to hit him over the head with.

Every part of me wants to show him what I'm really capable of. He's stepped over a solid line that I'd never intended to be crossed. I've never experienced this kind of crippling fury before. Something inside me has snapped, like a rubber band being stretched way too far.

This is too far.

I have the upper hand. I have always had the upper hand. Who does this fucker think he is? Nobody controls me. Certainly not him.

It's as if all the years of holding this darkness inside of me has finally begun to take its toll. I'm not a naïve girl to be toyed with; I'm a caged monster lost in all of time and space who has finally gotten the strength to break free.

Although I'm now blinking through blurred vision, I've never seen anything so clearly like this. My senses are heightened. My endorphins skyrocket at the fleeting thought of bashing his head in and making human Play-Doh out of his brain matter.

Michael leads me to his office and as soon as my gaze sets onto the paperweight resting on his desk, my heart leaps into the back of my throat. It taunts me. I'm suddenly starring in my own cartoon. I see tiny black hearts floating around the small, heavy object, and it calls out to me.

"Come play with me, Cora!" it sings to me.

"I don't see anything wrong with you," Nolan had told me.

The paperweight says it, too.

There's nothing wrong with you! This is how you were born!

The moment I pick it up from his desk, my heart swells. God, it feels so incredible against my palm. It fits so perfectly in my hand. It's like it was made for me.

It's as if I've fallen in love.

Give in to the madness! Embrace it! Set yourself free!

"Cora, no!" Michael shouts, dodging out of the way at just the right moment.

Well, shit. There goes that. The paperweight lands on the carpet with a dull thud. Fuming, I swipe my arm across his desk, knocking over the glass vase as it collides with the wall, shattering it into pieces.

"Fucking bastard!" I yell out, images of the deer crashing through my mind like bloody waves against the shore.

Chapter Fifteen

Nolan

Michael takes her away from the city and into the serene, upper-middle class township area where expensive houses sit tucked back deep in wooded estates surrounded by thick trees that blocks the view from the road. Winding hills and hidden drives begin to appear, and the cars thin out. I drop back, watching as he turns down one of these long driveways.

I park along the road, pulling my car into a thin scraggle of low hanging trees. It wasn't much, but it was enough cover to keep the car fairly hidden.

My phone buzzes as I'm creeping up the drive—gloves on, knife in hand—crouching low to keep out of view of the house's bright glow.

It's a new contact I never added.

Unknown: I think I might want to be unhealthy.

Unknown: Scratch that. I want to be a lunatic.

Well, there's only one person who would text me something like that.

Cora.

The house is a long, single story ranch home with blue shutters. I see a kids swing set in the back, along with a firepit and a trampoline. The image of Michael the predatory therapist is complete. A husband and family man with a respected career. It's clear that this is his night drive, his shadow life. Coercing the vulnerable and lording his power over them like a self-made God to women.

I hear muffled shouting in the home, stomping footsteps as the light flickers with shadows that pace back and forth.

The back door is locked; it makes a loud click when I turn the knob. I freeze, sure that I have been heard, but the voices simply rise in tenor.

There's a garage connected to the house. The side door is a flimsy, single lock that I manage to wedge a plastic shopping card between, releasing the mechanism. It pops open with a satisfying *clunk* and I'm in the dark garage, slinking along Michael's silver car. I hear more thunderous footsteps in the house; the sound of glass breaking.

I'm climbing the steps and about to enter through the kitchen when I see a long strand of rope hanging on the garage wall. I take it in my hands and grip it, pulling it taut.

A wonderful idea strikes me.

The kitchen is one of those minimalist Ikea designs that make it seem like no one actually lives there. It bothers me how much I like it. Flat stainless-steel countertops; glittering digital readouts on the microwave and oven. Everything is metal and gleaming. The cabinets are a dark wood and produce a soothing effect.

Somewhere in the house, I hear Cora yell, "Fucking bastard!"

I edge into the hallway, keeping close to the walls, my shoulder blades bumping family pictures and ski-trip collages. Michael the smiling father, Michael the cross-country skier, Michael dancing with a breezy, smiling woman who looks a bit like Natalie.

The living room features glass tables, a fireplace, an off-white carpet, and very few decorations. There's no dust, no paintings, and certainly no splash of color. No glasses half full linger on the coffee table. No magazines flipped halfway through. It would almost appear that a ghost lives here.

To think, I might have been Michael in another life.

Is that what hiding all the malice does? Hollows you out until your only thrill is seducing your patients?

How boring.

How...

Normal.

It is now very important to me that I kill this man, and not only that. I want to make him suffer.

Through the living room, into another hallway, and past a child's bedroom full of Lego toys, I hear Michael shouting. He's telling Cora to calm down, that this is just an episode she's having, and that she needs to contextualize her emotions and recognize she's having an "extreme response."

Cora's voice lowers to a breathy murmur, and I hear the rasp of clothing being taken off, and the sounds of kissing. Michael's tone shift from a pedantic voice to a gratified purr.

"Oh, really?" I hear him say. "That's how you want it?"

His voice makes me think of a pair of pliers I recently used in my own laundry room. I had to tighten a loose bolt that was making my dryer squeak. I am going to use the same pair to rip Michael's fingernails out.

There's a muffled thump. Michael groans and says, "Take it easy."

"Shut up. Don't move. Just let me... do... *this*."

Cora moans and I feel an awful, twisting pang of what must be jealousy. I lean into the room and see Cora, naked, her back to me as she rides Michael on the carpeted floor. She sinks herself down on him with a satisfied moan, and I see something golden glint in the soft yellow bedroom light.

An envelope opener; one of those gaudy, ridiculous blades that of course someone like Michael would have.

I watch as Cora raises the blade above her head while slowly rotating her hips, making Michael gasp, and then she slams the blade down, burying it into him.

He screams, but so does she. She throws her head back and cries out, leaning back until her head is nearly upside down, and in doing so, she sees me. A twisted, satisfied smile breaks across her face, and a thin line of drool drips from her mouth.

It is one of the scarier things I've ever seen.

She's stunning.

Michael chokes, and a large spurt of blood shoots out and hits the beige carpet. As I enter the room, I see that he's holding onto the blade, his mouth working soundlessly.

I approach Cora cautiously, gently touching the top of her head. "What did you do?"

She looks up at me, chest heaving, eyes bright. “I did it. I finally did it.”

Together, we look down at the envelope opener buried in his flesh, just above the collarbone. The only sound in the room is Cora’s harsh, unsteady breath.

I feel something tugging on my right hand, and I glance over to see that Cora has taken my hand and is holding it against her cheek. Some of Michael’s blood stains my fingers.

A pleasant silence hangs in the air. A calmness fills my mind and the gnashing malice that always seems to grip my brain dissipates.

“Is this how you feel?” she asks. “I feel... here. Present. That sense of time being flimsy is gone.” She flexes her hands, looking at them in wonder. “It’s like I have more blood in my body.”

I frown. He’s not dead, just in shock.

Kneeling next to her, I brush a sweaty strand of hair out of her face. She tilts her chin up at me and her eyes flicker back and forth across my own, searching for answers. “I don’t feel that. Whenever I kill—,” I grip the handle of the envelope opener and wrench it free with a wet *squelch.*”—it just quiets things down.”

Cora starts to say something else until Michael sits up and shrieks, clawing at the wound with both of his hands. Cora falls off him, her face a blank mask of shock as she scrambles backwards. He stands, one hand on the hilt of the blade, and the other swinging wildly in front of him.

His hair is crazed and sticking up in the back, and the whites of his eyes glare out at us as he backs away. His naked body looks pale and fragile, a steady line of blood oozing through the scraggly chest hairs and down his stomach.

Without warning, he reaches out for Cora.

Moving quickly, I pounce on him, driving one hand into his chest and knocking him back, the blood loss making him weak and unsteady. I pivot around behind him, grabbing the top of his hair and dragging him away.

"Don't you fucking touch her," I snap.

He groans and swings feebly at me, but whatever she hit with the blade has made him extremely weak. I laugh and knock his hands away, gathering them up and pinning them against his blood-drenched chest.

"Rope," I say to Cora.

"What?"

"The rope. Right there. I dropped it."

Shakily, she brings it over.

Michael writhes—his eyes glazed over—but he sees her and croaks, "Bitch. You fucking bitch."

I take my thumb and press it deep into the stab wound, feeling skin and tissue get caught under my fingernails, like when you dig your nails into a bar of soap.

"No, no, no! Please stop—"

Ignoring him, I turn my gaze to her. "Cora, would you be so kind as to tie his hands up for me?"

"My pleasure."

I hold his hands up to her and she loops the rope around them, cinching them together and winding them up in an intricate knot. I smile at her handiwork.

"Such a good girl. Now I'm going to take him with me. I need you to clean up here. Can you do that?"

She nods. Her eyes have been widening this entire time, as if she's coming down from whatever high the stabbing had produced and reckoning with what she has done.

"It's going to be okay," I tell her.

"I know. I'm fine."

"Of course, you are. I just need you to focus and make sure it looks like he ran off. It doesn't have to be perfect. It just needs to buy us time."

"Okay."

Michael has fallen quiet. Blood oozes steadily from the wound, shining wetly in the soft yellow light of the bedroom. I rack my brain, trying to figure out how to get him out of the house and into my car without leaving a trail of blood behind.

Cora disappears for a moment and reappears with a thick plastic blue tarp and several bungee cords.

"Will this work?"

I nod.

She shakes the tarp out flat, and together we tip his slumped form onto it, laying him out face down. We begin pulling the edges and corners over him, covering him in the plastic, and cinching it closed with the bungee cords. The blood stops leaking onto the carpet, and only his head remains uncovered.

"Should we put a bag on his head or something?" Cora asks.

"No. Let's sit him up."

We pull him back up, leaning his back against the end of the bed as he sits on the floor. His eyes flutter open, and he looks at us with disgust.

"You're going to get caught," Michael says. "You're going to rot in a cell." He glares at me. "You're just like her, aren't you? A freak. You're not even human."

Cora and I stand over him, and for the first time I'm fully aware of how naked she is. I had been caught up in the bloodlust, but now the back of my hand is touching her bare hip, and I can hear her breathing next to me.

I want her so bad.

"Why aren't we covering his face?"

"Because I want him to watch."

"Watch what?" she asks, but I'm already pulling her against me, my hands grabbing her ass and squeezing it as hard as I can.

She returns the favor by sinking her teeth into my shoulder. The pain pisses me off, just a little, and I reach up and grab her by the hair, forcing her to the ground in front of Michael. I lay her on her back, her hair splayed out behind her head on the carpet. She giggles, and lazily looks over at him. Sinking to my knees next to her, I take one of her hands and direct it down her body, stopping between her thighs.

I lean in and mutter, "Play with yourself. Let us watch."

"Oh? Is that what you want?" She slowly begins to caress herself, rubbing her clit with a delicate, slow intensity. "I don't think he deserves to watch though..."

My hand joins hers, my middle and ring finger sliding into her while she begins working her hand faster.

"He doesn't," I state. "But let him see what he'll never get to touch again."

"You're both sick. Please. This hasn't gone too far yet. I think you're both in a manic, high-energy state and—"

With my fingers I spread Cora's pussy apart, letting a long line of saliva fall onto it. Then I look directly into Michael's eyes as I begin sinking my fingers in and out of her, feeling her clench around me. Michael growls something and squeezes his eyes shut.

"Open your eyes," Cora orders him. "Open your eyes and watch what he does to me."

The anger and firmness of her tone makes my pulse quicken. I lift her up slightly and take her in my mouth, my tongue sliding into her, flicking and twisting against her clit. Her nails dig into the back of my head as she begins bucking her hips against me, grinding against my mouth. I withdraw and kiss the inside of her thighs, running my lips all over her slick pussy before diving back in, gathering more saliva in my mouth and using it to make her even wetter.

"Open your eyes!"

I sit up, Cora's wetness on my chin, and look over. Michael is sitting firmly with his eyes closed, his head tilted away. Grinning at Cora, I lean in to kiss her jaw.

"I'll take care of it. Keep touching yourself for me."

She licks her lips and moves her hand back down between her legs.

I go over to Michael, who's struggling back and forth in his bonds. One of the bungee cords around his neck is straining and threatening to come loose. I tighten it up for him.

"Michael, you know, I have some pliers. A great pair of pliers. They have this grip on the handle; it is just *sublime.* Now, I'll be honest, I was going to rip your fingernails out with them, because frankly I think they can get a good hold. A firm hold, really. But..." I tug on the bungee cord. The plastic crinkles as Michael wriggles to get away from me. "If you don't watch what I do to Cora, I will peel the skin off your face and make you eat it." I get so close to him we're nearly kissing. I can see the sweat beading in his pores.

"Yes! Peel the skin off his face, Nolan!" Cora chants from behind me.

"You're going to watch while I make her gag on my cock. You're gonna watch when I bend her over in front of you. Then I'll make sure you're listening to her moan my name while I take her on your office floor. Most of all? You will hear her beg me for more." I grab his face in both of my hands, pressing my forehead to his. "And I know, I *know* you're bleeding pretty bad. I *know* you feel possessive of Cora. But she is mine and if you don't do what I say, Michael—if you don't do what I say? *Your family will weep when they see what I've done to you.*"

I watch him struggle, opening his mouth to speak, not trusting the words he comes up with. This is a man of words; a sense of structure and worth derived from academia, ideas, citations and sources. All of that is stripped away and he can only avert his gaze from mine, those glittering sentences useless in a game of blood and power.

I meander back to Cora. The wild thing in her has already found its way onto all fours and is crawling to me, her hands roaming up my body as she reaches me, tugging at my shirt and urging me to take off my clothes. I pull the fabric over my head and feel her undoing my pants, fumbling with the zipper, licking her lips and glancing up at me. I tuck her hair gently behind her head and lock eyes with Michael.

"Look how bad she wants it."

Cora's hands are warm and firm on my cock as she sits on her knees and strokes it with both hands. She leans forward and licks it, running her tongue slowly up the length of the shaft, before drawing back and licking the head briefly with the tip of her tongue, looking up at me and laughing. Her breath is hot and sudden on my skin. She pulls me closer, about to swallow it fully, until I cup her chin with my palm and tilt her head up to me instead.

"Beg for it," I tell her softly.

For the briefest second, her eyes narrow, and I realize I have forgotten she is a threat; all of this is a risk. Stabbing Michael, getting involved with something as volatile as Cora, the entire thing could so easily come crashing down around me. I should bolt; leave Cora to deal with her own chaos, and I could disappear into the American abyss, reappear as someone else, and slate my bloodthirst in such a way that would allow me to continue as long as I desired. This is how you get caught. Being careless, being involved, being *known*.

The pause hangs in the air, Cora's annoyed gaze fixes upon me, and I realize she's not going to do it, and that even if we manage to move past this and keep fucking, the spell will be broken, and I'll be able to escape her. Her struggle between resisting me and punishing him will end. She'll quit this contest of bluffs and retreats, of seeing how far the other will go. The game will end, and I will be free.

Then Michael scoffs.

She swivels her head, surveying him with a passive expression on her face. Something clicks for her, because she turns and hits me with a smoldering look and crawls even closer, her mouth hanging open and eyes wide in an expression of pleading desire.

"Please," she whispers, just loud enough for him to hear it. "Please let me have it."

"Oh, that's not loud enough, princess. Beg. Louder."

There's a split second when that lethal Cora-rage appears on her face, telling me I'm likely to pay for calling her that, but she fights it back and presses her lips to the underside of my cock, tilting her head back so that she can maintain eye contact with me while having it rest against her face.

"Please, can I suck your dick?" she asks, the movement of her lips causing tickling friction that makes me grin. She starts talking faster. "Please stick it in my mouth, sir. Please fuck my face. Choke me with your big, thick cock. I want it. I want to be your *whore.* Fuck me in front of him, use me however you want, I just want it so fucking bad—"

Her words are cut off as I savagely shove my cock in her mouth, making her gag as it brushes the back of her throat, but I don't relent.

I pull her hair tightly back with both hands, shoving my cock in as far as it will go, as one of her hands grip the back of my calf tightly. One of her feet beats the ground behind her. I pull out and she gasps, drool leaking all over Michael's floor.

"Please," she groans, breathless, and I can't tell if she's begging for mercy as her mouth is on my cock again or begging for more until her mouth tightens around it, grazing me lightly with her teeth as she drags her tongue along it, forcing my length deeper and deeper into her throat.

I have her hair in a ponytail, and I pull back on it, urging her to slow her pace.

"Take it slow, baby," I tell her. "I want to watch you."

I grin at Michael as her head bobs in slow, sensuous fashion, her tongue lathering my cock, coating it in saliva.

"How about it? Are you watching, too?"

To his credit, he does hold my gaze steadily for a moment before he flickers down and watches Cora work. I groan, playing it up just to mess with him. I have both of my hands laced behind her head as she sucks.

"She must really hate you," I say pleasantly to him, "because this feels *incredible.*"

She moans with me in her mouth, and the vibration sends me to heaven. I assume she can feel my hands tightening around her head because she stops sucking just as I'm about to burst and gets to her feet. Reaching along my hips she grasps my cock and strokes it, coiling it against me. "Do you know what I want?"

"Hmm, what's that, princess?"

"I want you to bend me over in front of him. I want him to look me in the eyes while you make me come."

"Oh, come on," Michael mutters.

It's faint, but I hear it. I don't blame him; what he's watching me do to Cora is tearing him apart. And I'm not even sure who is in control at this moment, because Cora is leading me over to him, sinking to her knees, straddling his bound legs, reaching out and caressing his cheek. Coyly, she leans forward showing off her ass to me while one of her hands reaches between her legs and draws a finger deep inside of her cunt. She looks back at me, the color in her eyes seeming to dance in the light.

"Well, are you gonna fuck me? Or do I have to beg again?" She laughs, short and bitter. "Fine." She looks straight at Michael, inches from his face. "Please, Nolan. Please fuck me."

Chapter Sixteen

Cora

I expect Nolan to be rough. I want it. Need it. I want him to claim me in front of Michael, make me tremble and moan with uncontrollable pleasure. In this moment he can do whatever he wants to me, whatever sick perverted things he has lurking in the twisted corridors of his mind. I'm entirely his, his object, his toy.

But instead of sliding into me immediately and pounding away, he surprises me by kissing up my back, starting just above my hips and trailing up my spine, firm, warm kisses with just a hint of tongue, making me shiver deliciously with each one. He reaches the back of my neck and lingers there, kissing each side of it, his lips brushing against my left ear, and then my right. I feel him smile against my neck as he moves some of my hair away.

I hear him sigh when he thrusts into me in one, long stroke. His arms wrap around me and pull me closer to him, his hands gently around my neck and holding my face, turning me around slightly so he can observe as he starts to fuck me with slow, easy thrusts, teasing me as he slowly builds up speed.

"Oh, *God*," I groan. I begin pushing back on him and for a moment I forget entirely about Michael as Nolan's breathing quickens.

The game disappears for a moment when he says, “Fuck, please keep doing that. You feel so good. Please.”

Something about having him say “please” in my ear brings me to a shuddering orgasm and I cry out, closing my eyes and pushing back on his cock, waves of pleasure cascading through, Nolan’s voice breaking into a hoarse whisper as he says over and over, “Keep going baby, keep going, keep coming for me—“

And then Michael moves, the plastic crinkling, shattering the illusion, ruining the moment. Ruining *everything*.

We stop for a moment, both Nolan and I. Both of us gaze at Michael with homicidal fury.

Then Nolan grabs a fistful of my hair and yanks it back, and begins fucking me as hard as he can, the veins popping out in his forearms. He aims my face directly at Michael as I bite my lip in ecstasy.

“You’re lucky her pussy feels this good,” Nolan growls at him, “or I’d kill you right now.”

The word “kill” flickers in my mind and suddenly I’m on the verge again, staring into Michael’s eyes, making sure he sees, making sure he *knows* how hard I’m coming and the only reason it’s possible is Nolan.

Nolan

I'm pretty tired while dragging Michael to the car.

The quivering lump of human is entirely dead weight. He hasn't said anything, even when I made Cora swallow my cum in front of him. This pleases me; it means he believed my threats.

I never wanted to be one of those serial killers who don't have the gift of menace. It was easy to be one of the sulking, greasy losers who killed people to lash out at a world that didn't understand them. There were plenty of those. I held myself to a different standard. I wanted to be something that transcended television screens. Something heinous to blight the eye of an entire world.

Michael gets to be a part of that, and I'm so, so pleased.

Things have accelerated, going far beyond what I was prepared for. I was going to plan for years. *Years,* can you believe it? All that waiting, all the planning, all that Natalie, Natalie, Natalie, and for what? Why not just rip the mask off and bite into the world now? It was going to end badly. It was *always* going to end badly, either in death or a cell.

A cell, a cell. I had to be careful, to avoid the cell.

An image flashes of iron bars in my head, and I recoil from it in disgust. My boredom rips at me even now, a cell will unravel me. I have to have so many bodies.

The dream of the house resurfaces. They need to pull up the floorboards of my life, my career, and find bodies, twisted and mangled. Michael will be in the basement. Michael in the foundations. Michael in neat little pieces, stuffed under the staircase.

He's heavier than I expected. I drag him easily through the kitchen, his flesh gliding smoothly across the gleaming tile floor. I prop the door to the garage open with a blue bag of rock salt, and pull him down the small staircase, his head clunking and lolling around as it jostles down each step.

Keys.

I lean him against the back bumper of his car. His eyes flutter and his mouth twitches. I flick his nose, and he startles awake.

"Wha—?"

"Where are your keys?"

"Why would I tell you?"

I squeeze his face between my fingers. "I'm going to eat your fucking liver."

I stomp back into the kitchen, back through the living room. No keys. Where does he keep them? I circle the house before finally going into the bedroom.

Cora had been exhausted after our fun in front of Michael and fell asleep on his bed. She lay on her stomach, her naked shoulders uncovered.

The keys are on the bedside table. I grab them and am about to turn to leave when I stop and cover her up with the blanket.

The old shipping yard is a sea of jagged, rusted metal, stuck into the muddy earth like crooked teeth embedded into rotting gums. A twisting labyrinth of dead locomotive cars, shipping containers and tankers, discarded and left to degrade. There'd been a river flowing through, maybe ten years ago, but it had dried up to a shallow creek. The paper factories dried up too, leaving behind acres of dead metal.

It creaks and groans in the wind as I drag Michael out of the car, the sheets of metal warbling with each gust.

It's a shame I won't be able to keep using this lovely blue container. I find it soothing; opening its clanging door, hearing the chains rattle and clunk as I unlock it. I feel like a monster returning to its cave; a vampire slipping into its coffin.

It is an entire world of my design.

Grunting, I hoist him onto the table. His hair is matted to his skull; his lips have turned an ashy white. The blood has clotted where Cora stabbed him, and there's a swirling, disconnected moment as I stare at it.

In the grocery store I'd see the meat packaged and sealed. The plastic pressing against the flesh, and, on some of the steaks, a thin residue of blood. I'd stare at that blood, tantalized by it, hungry for it.

Michael's chest looks like meat; like multiple shades of crimson pressed together like paint mixing on an easel.

I'm a kid with a new friend over and I have to show him all my new toys.

Quickly, I tape him to the table. He struggles, but is weak, and I have to keep slapping him to keep him awake.

"You're gonna miss it! You're gonna miss it!"

Tape, tape, tape. Around and around and around. One runs dry, the adhesive pulling all the way down to the cardboard roll. I unwrap another, then another. The shipping container is a cacophony of noise; every breath, footstep, and crackle of plastic echoes flatly off the walls, returned to me in tinny accusation. It's as if I'm on a stage, an audience before me, gasping at my actions.

Michael is secured on the table, his head rolling back and forth. I wander around him, pulling my gloves fully onto my hands.

"Remember, I had a pair of pliers picked out for this, but then Cora went and stabbed you so...," I shrug. "The best laid plans, you know."

On one of the stacked plastic totes lies a collection of utensils, neatly in a row like filed teeth, ready to shred him. I pick up a scalpel; I scavenged it from a biology class, years ago, and never had the joy of using it.

I hold his head tightly with one hand, pressing down on his forehead, wrinkling the skin.

"Please," he croaks. His eyes tilt upward, looking into mine. My hair hangs over him; I must look like a homicidal caricature, frenzied and delighted.

"You don't understand what you mean to me," I tell him.

I delicately pluck at one of his eyelids, hearing a light *puck* sound as it unsticks from his eye.

"I'm building a house, you see. Metaphorical and wonderful."

The scalpel digs into the soft, gummy flesh of the eyelid, his lashes crushing and splintering apart, a few fluttering down and landing on his cheek. He weakly cries out, and starts to turn his head, but the scalpel catches and drags further, making him howl in agony.

"This house of corpses starts with you," I say softly. "You're one of my first." I sever the eyelid in a quick motion, cutting from the bridge of his nose over to the side of his eye socket.

The scalpel makes a dry *grrrk* sound when it hits bone. Michael sits up as much as he can and unleashes a scream that vibrates my eardrums; I can hear it shaking the walls of the shipping container.

I slap the top of his head and force him back down. His bare eye glares at me, and I find it kind of frightening. The side of his face is coated in blood. I wipe it away with a rag and start on the other eye.

"No-no-no-no-*no!*" Michael is beside himself, quaking in terror. I hear something dripping and look up to see a thin line of yellow urine extending from the silver of the tabletop to the floor below.

This is so sloppy. I should have coated the walls in tarps. This will take forever to clean.

The second eyelid is cleaner; it's like cutting wrapping paper. You have to pull the skin taught and get the blade to *glide.*

I take both eyelids and place them on the tips of my fingers and waggle them in front of Michael.

He doesn't like this.

There's too much blood on his face and that bothers me, so I place the eyelids on the tray of tools and clean him up with a rag.

More blood gushes out, filling his eyes.

"I'm sorry," I tell him. "I didn't think there was that much in there!"

I cut some of the tape and turn him to his side, where he chokes and sputters, shaking his head, blood spattering onto the table and floor.

This isn't going smoothly, but it is so exciting.

Leaning one of the totes is a metal baseball bat. It glints in the dim battery powered lights, catching my eye. Between Cora's stab, and the shock of what I've done, he's probably going to pass out or die soon.

There's never enough time to do what I want.

"You took advantage of her."

"Please—"

I grip the bat, rotating my wrists and swinging it around, then set it against the table. I scoop up the detached eyelids. I flatten them in my palm, flaying them out. They look like wet, limp, flesh-colored potato-chips.

I kneel in front of Michael's wide, jack-o-lantern gaze. I can see how much eyes move now, bouncing back and forth in the socket like pinballs.

"You abused your power," I shout in his face, pinching his nose shut and stuffing the eyelids in his mouth. "Chew," I order in a simple, disinterested voice.

He whimpers.

"Chew," I whisper.

He gags but does as he's told, still chewing when I start hitting him with the bat.

A while later—and I do mean a *while*—I'm shirtless, sweating, and very frustrated. The temperature in the shipping container seems to have doubled. I've taken off my belt because it was digging into my waist as I leaned over the table. My forearms are glistening with sweat and my shoulders are aching because of the angle I'm leaning at.

Michael's face still refuses to separate from his skull.

I had an idea on how to do it. A thin knife slicing a line under the throat, cutting with short, severe strokes, tilting the knife so it digs into the skin.

From there, simply circle his entire face with the knife, slip under the skin, sever a tendon or two, and it'll slide right off.

I kept thinking it'd be like a soft tortilla shell. I would be able to scrunch it together into my fist and rip it away.

The muscles around his mouth cling to the skin. I peel it back a bit and begin sawing at it, but the blood keeps pouring out of the wound, welling up and spilling onto the table in thick spatters.

You could always sew it back together.

That's an idea. I can break his head apart and have a better angle to chisel flesh away. It need not be a full skinning; if I could get big enough chunks of skin, I could create a nice patchwork quilt of dead flesh.

And then give it to Cora.

She did say that she always wondered how it would feel to be in someone's skin.

I pull Michael's limp head to the side of the table, hanging him over the edge, face down. His skull bobbles slightly but settles still. It looks like a baseball on a tee.

I stretch my shoulders as I stroll among my tools, before settling on the sledgehammer. My hands circle around the handle and I grunt to hoist it over my shoulder. Michael is leaking blood onto the floor.

I align my feet in front of him, framing the back of his head with my toes. As I bring the hammer over my head, Michael utters a shuddering, horrific gasp.

Humans are so resilient.

I miss a bit with the hammer. Instead of hitting dead center—just above the nape of his neck—I connect to the right. The wood handle vibrates in my hands as the head deflects off his skull, a nasty sound echoing in the shipping container.

Thuck.

I try again. It's like cooking. You make mistakes, but the key is to make them into *delicious* mistakes.

The second blow is too far toward the crown of Michaels head. It snaps his neck as he is forced to nod viciously forward, the remaining teeth in his head rattling on the ground as they fall out.

Alright, one more time.

The third swing of the hammer splits his head apart, and I see a flash of his delightful grey brain, pulsing for a shining moment before the blood can fill the gap.

I think of split apples, pumpkins smashed against the ground, watermelons and cantaloupes bashed apart, eggs broken in the carton.

I stick a bucket underneath him to catch some of the blood, then I lean on the hammer, watching him bleed while I catch my breath.

I've destroyed his head. Some of the skin won't be salvageable.

But...

Soon there will be more victims. More skin. Jerald is rotting in a barrel, but there should be some skin loosened by deterioration that I can take and weave into Michael's.

You could pin it all on her.

The thought sneaks in with crafty ease. Cora will have a mask of all *her* victims. She has connections to Jerald and Michael. Motive, even.

And she's too unbalanced to make the right moves, to react quickly enough.

How easy would it be to kill another victim with her along for the ride... maybe two. Let her play alongside me, see how good of a little monster she could be.

Then slip out, direct the police to her, disappear.

We could use Michael's house as a base for now. It's Thursday night; Michael has no appointments on Friday or through the weekend. I imagine that's why he was so keen on getting Cora alone for a while. His wife and kids are on vacation for another week at Disney World. He gets to play the heroic, hardworking father, *sacrificing* so his family can enjoy themselves. And he can take care of his patients.

Maybe I could email his office, tell them he was taking an impromptu vacation.

That would buy us time.

Fuck Cora a few more times, kill a few more people, then leave. Ditch everything. Become someone else.

I'm innocent, after all.

Build her into a serial killer, egg her on until she's completely unhinged, and then slip off into glorious obscurity to continue the bloodshed.

There's a flashing image of myself, sitting in a dark room, a singular lightbulb over my head as I studiously work a thread a needle through flaps of dried, pale skin.

The feeling it gives me is the same feeling I imagine old folks feel about sitting serenely on their porches while knitting a blanket on a summer morning.

Relaxation.

I'm sure Cora will love this. And if someone ever asks me what my love language is, I can give them a genuine, heartfelt smile.

Why, it's gift giving, of course.

Chapter Seventeen

Nolan

I'm discovering that there's a routine to cleaning after a kill. Even a particular joy to be found. It is soothing, a sense of everything falling into the right place. As a child I enjoyed jigsaw puzzles, relishing the mild catharsis each time a piece fit snugly against its true other. Order.

After a kill, an eerie calmness pours over my body, and the routine is an extension of this. The shipping container is a perfectly segmented, compartmentalized aspect of my life, and the cleanup reflects that.

The table is stripped of all plastic and duct tape. Any debris left over from the body is deftly swept into a garbage bag. The floors, covered in a tightly orchestrated series of tarps and sealed plastic, are ripped up, everything balled up and tucked into garbage bags. I roll a pressure-washer into the container and slowly work my way around the entirety, blasting the steel sides with soap and water. The walls will begin to rust, eventually, but by then I'll have moved on. A new location. A new routine.

The rolls of garbage bags and plastic wrap go into tidy little plastic bins and get tucked into the corner. Whatever tools I use are rinsed off with the power washer and stored in another bin.

It amuses me that, a few short hours ago, I was gleefully stabbing a man in the chest, his screams echoing off the harsh steel of the container, and now it looks pristine. I no longer need to night drive and hunt down wounded deer. I have this new life, this crimson mask to slip on at my leisure.

I'm blissful in these thoughts as I strip off the pants I have on and toss them into one of the bags. There's a change of clothes waiting in my gym bag, but for the moment it is nice to feel the cool air on my bare skin. I relish these moments of tranquility.

There's a noise at the door. A scraping sound. Someone is picking the lock.

Police would have barged in, yelling, with lights and sirens.

Someone looking for the victim would've knocked or called out.

So, who would be creeping around, trying to get the drop on me?

I grab one of the knives and snap the lights off, slinking back into the darkness of one of the corners. The container door pulls open a bit, and a flashlight clicks on. Someone steps through the gap and starts shining the light around. My eyes adjust to the darkness and make use of the light reflecting off the steel walls.

Cora.

All the talk, all the mind games, all the confrontation, and now she's here, waving a flashlight around like she's daring me to take her.

She moves to the center of the room, scanning the table with the light. She'd said we were more alike than I knew. If that were true, she would notice me. If that were true, her instincts would have sensed me, lurking in the shadows, watching her.

I'm reaching out and grabbing her, one arm hooking around her throat, the other pinning her arms to her sides, when it occurs to me that maybe she wants to be caught. Everything is a game, a challenge, a test. Why would this be any different?

"You shouldn't be here," I say in her ear, trying to ignore the sudden quickening of my pulse as I inhale the citrus smell of her shampoo. There's an attraction here I am uncomfortable with. Most of the time, all of the time, I feel cold and reptilian, with only vague notions of wants and needs.

But with Cora, I want her. I want to play the game. I want things to escalate. I want them to get better, get worse, descend into chaos. I want her to destroy me, and rebuild me just to destroy me again, as I struggle to do the same to her.

She tilts her face upward, her cheek pressing against mine.

"I'm in your *lair*," she teases. "What are you going to do about it?"

I shove her against the table, pressing her face down onto the cold steel. "How did you find me?"

"I tracked Michael's car."

I hold her there for a moment, relishing the way her ass is pressed against me, the curve of her back as her shirt rides up and reveals the soft, smooth, skin of her lower back. I want to kiss it, but instead I walk around the table, click the lights back on, and kneel so my face is next to hers. She remains bent over, waiting for what I have in store for her.

"Do you know what I do to people in here?" I ask her, pushing the strands of her hair out of her eyes.

She meets my gaze and smiles. "I don't really care what you do to them." She licks her lips. "I'm more interested in what you're going to do to me."

"Don't move."

I straighten up and walk to the bins and pull out the tape, the plastic, and the knives. I should kill her. That is the clearest, most calculated answer. She has tracked me this far, and knows what I am. No amount of personal connection is worth the risk she poses.

I hear something clink, and the rustle of clothing. As I turn around, I see that Cora has stripped off her clothing and is sitting on top of the table in a white bra and black panties. Her legs are spread slightly as she leans back on her hands and grins at me.

I really, really need to kill her.

I cross the room holding the knives and plastic, but she doesn't flinch.

"I told you not to move," I say quietly.

One of her bare feet rises up and gently caresses the crotch of my boxer briefs. I notice the faded, peeling turquoise nail polish.

"You don't seem to mind," she says, tilting her chin at my growing erection, straining against the fabric.

The smile on her face is cut off as I grab her by the throat, slamming her down onto the table with a heavy *clang* as the metal buckles slightly from the force. Her hands wrap around my wrist tightly, but she's not prying my fingers away, and that fucking smile hasn't left her face.

Kill her now, Nolan. Do it.

I frown; I rarely have inner thoughts. I'm never of two minds about anything. I am honed and focused; more of a sentient ballistic missile than a man.

So why the hesitation? Why the gnawing curiosity as to how far this will go? Every survival instinct is sounding the alarm, a thudding pulse rising in my ears, a low voice deep in the recesses of my mind telling me to put this fire out, now, before it spreads and torches the entire forest, burning down the entirety of Nolan.

The knife is still in my right hand as I loom over her. Her eyes watch it for a moment, then flick over and meet my gaze. Daring me.

I press the blade to her neck, fascinated with the way her body tenses, the veins appearing on the sides of her throat, the slight widening of her eyes, and her smile fading ever-so-slightly. My face is a remorseless mask; I refuse to give her any hint of my intentions. Cora confuses me. Excites me. Interests me. But that falls apart the moment one of us stops playing the game.

I trail the flat side of the knife down her collarbone, dragging the tip firmly against her skin, drifting along the curve of one of her breasts, watching the blade press into her flesh, daring it to break open and begin to bleed.

I wonder if she has any idea of the danger she is in. I'm certain that if I see blood in this moment, I will lose control and the game will end in stunning, glorious violence.

The knife slips under each bra strap, and with a firm tug it cuts cleanly through, the white cups falling loosely to the side as I cut it off her, my hand never leaving her throat.

My grip loosens slightly though, and she mutters, "Are you going to stab me or fuck me, Nolan?"

I release her neck to cover her mouth with my palm, her lipstick smearing against my hand—it is still wet, she applied it for my benefit—and turning her head away from me. The sudden movement makes her legs kick out, the table clanging once again. Still holding the knife in the other hand, I pin one of her legs down. Her thrashing causes the blade to nick her, a thin red scratch appearing on her inner thigh. I freeze, staring at it, painfully aware that I've never been this aroused in my life. Not with Natalie, not with anyone.

The voice telling me to kill her and run has gotten quieter, and when I lean down and put my lips to the scratch, finally tasting the soft warmth of her skin, the voice is blissfully silent. I kiss up and down her thigh, starting at her knee and working upwards, letting just a hint of my tongue touch her until I get to the scratch again, and then I lick it fully, my tongue flat and hot as I trace the entire length of it.

She grabs the back of my head, gathering a fistful of my hair, thrusting her hips upward toward me, but I shake her off.

"Not yet."

She glares at me and I almost smile. It occurs to me that I am having fun. Knife still in hand, I begin slowly, gently rubbing her over the flimsy cotton underwear she's wearing. She's soaked, and the thin bit of fabric is such a tease. I increase the pressure, using my index and ring finger to spread her lips apart under the panties, my middle finger firm against her clit, stroking up and down, working in tight, determined circles. I wonder briefly if I'm hitting the right spot, a bolt of some feeling that must be insecurity.

Why does she do this to me?

Suddenly Cora is raising herself up on her elbows, her breath hitching, her moans rising in pitch, and getting more and more breathless.

"Faster, please, faster," she murmurs, and that's when I remove my hand completely, stepping away and grabbing the roll of plastic. A look of pure rage and frustration darkens on her face as she watches me.

"Do not stop."

It is not a question. It is a command, only I'm not her boyfriend, or any of her playthings. I ignore her and drag her to her feet, pulling her around by her hair like she is my pet.

"Put your arms to your sides. Tight."

She bites her tongue, still glaring at me, but doing as she's told. I take the roll and stretch out the plastic, starting just above her shoulders and wrapping it downward in a slow spiral, trapping her arms against her body, the plastic squeezing her breasts together as I wrap it tighter and tighter.

I get on my knees in front of her and slide her panties down, looking up at her as I do so, my lips trailing lightly down the front of her stomach, stopping *just* before I reach her pussy.

The plastic creaks as she strains against it. "Eat shit, Nolan."

I laugh and proceed to wind around her with the roll of plastic wrap, pinning her legs together, covering her waist, her thighs, her ass. Soon she is cocooned in sterile, orderly plastic. A neat package for me to do whatever I want with. I circle behind her, examining her, when she totters backwards into me. I catch her, and suddenly we're face to face.

"What now?" she taunts.

I run my hand down the front of her, listening to the plastic creak and squeal.

"I'm not sure," I say softly. "Normally if I wrap someone up, they're in several pieces. And they don't talk."

She nuzzles against my neck, her lips warm and soft as she kisses me. "But now you have a mouthy little girl all tied up. You could do anything you want to me, and I couldn't stop you."

I can't take it anymore.

I spin her around and lift her, tossing her over my shoulder. I flip her back onto the table, the metal legs sliding on the floor. I roll her onto her stomach, her head hanging off the side, her black hair disheveled and hanging in her eyes. I pull down my pants and shove my cock into her mouth, holding the back of her head with both hands as I thrust. She begins gagging, saliva dripping lazily onto the floor. I reach out and bring my hand down as hard as I can on her ass, over and over, and each time I do she moans with my dick in her mouth. The sensation is maddening. She is mine. Helpless and begging for it, she is mine.

I groan loudly as I come, and Cora's tongue starts working faster as I do, making my knees buckle as a wave of pleasure hits me.

I withdraw from her mouth abruptly. She turns her head and smiles again, my cum white and contrasting against her smeared, sloppy lipstick.

"That can't be it," she says.

I turn away from her briefly, back to the bin with the plastic and tools. I have small, black bags that I use to cover victims' faces. I grab one of these and cross the room back to Cora, kneeling in front of her.

"Not even close," I reply. I throw the bag over her head, suffocating her.

"Nolan, what—"

She tries to inhale a breath, the bag crinkling with her struggle as her body begins to flail. Although she finds no oxygen, and after several seconds, her panic is evident.

"Nolan," she chokes.

Her erratic gasps and horrified whimpers become more frequent and louder as time passes. At the very last second, before her body goes limp, I shove my finger through the plastic, granting her air.

It takes her a while to catch her breath before she growls at me viciously. "What the fuck was that?"

Clamping my hand over her mouth, I cut her words off. "You will be silent. Nod your head if you understand."

Against my grip, she snarls, "You could have fucking killed me!"

"Yet, you're still here, aren't you?"

She says nothing.

Cora is quiet, trying to decipher her thoughts while I get dressed. I will have to come back and clean the container, but for now it should be fine. I open the door and glance around for witnesses, but the night is silent and warm.

I pick Cora up again and carry her to my car. I throw her into the backseat, lock the shipping container, and drive off, trying my best not to speed. I want to get home and play with my toy, but the difficulty of trying to explain to a police officer why I have a woman wrapped in plastic in my backseat is too much even for me. So, I use my blinkers and stop at every light, wondering what I am going to do to her when I get home.

Chapter Eighteen

Cora

It takes everything in me to not speak a word during the ride to wherever Nolan plans on taking me. His apartment? A cemetery, where he can dig a hole and toss me into it? He could have just killed me back in his lair, except he didn't. Does he plan on edging me, after getting me all worked up, and burying me alive instead?

Suddenly, I feel myself imagining how that must feel. Lying in the cold, damp dirt, surrounded by bugs, twigs, and rocks, staring up at the night sky as dirt flies through the air and lands on my naked body. Caressing my skin. Packing me further into the ground. Making me just another small, unimportant part of the earth.

How would it feel to have a mouthful of dirt? Why is it that I know *exactly* what it would feel like? Somehow, I can taste it on my tongue. I can feel the way it alters my breathing, tiny clumps of dirt clogging my nostrils and packing down my throat.

Yeah.

Being buried alive would be a hell of a way to go.

I've never been one to obey orders. Rules have never applied to me before. Not in this lifetime, at least. And now, here I am, keeping my mouth shut and doing exactly as Nolan has instructed, bound in plastic and breathing through a small hole in the bag that's secured over my head.

He has this bizarre hold on me. Maybe it's because he's the first person who has ever understood me. He doesn't even have to try.

He just *does*.

"You could have killed me back there, but you didn't," I speak up, breaking my silence. "Is it because you're planning on killing me somewhere else? Your lair wasn't good enough? Or do you just plan on fucking me some more?"

"I told you to be quiet," he snaps.

"Ah. You don't plan on fucking me, then. Killing, it is," I sigh. "Unfortunate. I was really looking forward to it. We have so much chemistry."

"Shut your fucking mouth, Cora," he growls over me.

"If I do that, then I won't be able to suck your dick."

"There won't be any need for that," he sadistically replies. "I'll be having too much fun fucking the gaping stab wound in your stomach. Warm, and squishy. And self-lubricated. Made just for me."

"That's hot," I moan, wetting my lips with my tongue.

"You're a sick, twisted little freak," he groans, taking a sudden sharp turn. "You know that?"

His apartment is like walking into a furniture store display. It's sparsely decorated, with tidy black and white rugs on the floor. There's no TV, no books lining the walls. No coffee cup casually sitting on the counter. I turn my head around, craning my neck to look at everything as I'm carried through the door and down the hall, his arms holding me tightly over the curve of his shoulder.

He pushes through another door into his bedroom and tosses me carelessly onto a bed with gray sheets. I roll on them, enjoying how they smell faintly of his spiced cologne, the one that reminds me of dark rum and cedar trees, before sitting up and looking around his room.

Again, like an Ikea ad. No photos on the bedside table. No posters or hanging sports flags. A small desk lurks in the corner, a jacket hung over the back of the chair.

What catches my eye is the painting he has hanging up on the wall across from the bed. A vacant white canvas, large, hung deliberately within view as he would fall asleep. A singular, red dot in the center of it.

I could imagine him lying there each night, staring at the red as the murderous abyss swirled behind his eyes.

He flips me onto my stomach and rips the plastic at my legs, giving him access. My body trembles with excitement as I feel the sharp tip of a blade pressing against the sensitive skin between my thighs, cutting the plastic wrap evenly down the middle, exposing me to him. I shudder with anticipation, waiting for the unknown.

Everything he does is unexpected. Finally, I found someone just as batshit crazy as I am. Completely unhinged, in the most beautiful of ways.

He lets out a sharp, enthusiastic breath as he rests the flat side of the knife against my thigh, urging me to spread my legs for him. My legs spread wide on their own accord.

"Where did you come from, Cora?" he asks me, grazing the cold flat surface of the blade against my clit. A shiver travels down my spine.

"Same as you, Nolan," I answer with a hushed moan, grinding my pussy against his knife. "The darkest corner of the coldest depth of hell."

Suddenly, something is inside of me. And it's not the knife. It's not him, either. Whatever it is, it's extremely hard. Cold. *Lifeless*.

Nolan eases the object into me as deep as my body allows. I'm soaking wet. I try to break my arms free from the plastic wrap, except it's no use. Instead, I arch my back and use my hips to rock back and forth on the bed. I cry out to him, throwing back my ass and meeting each forceful thrust with a hunger so powerful, I'm not sure anyone or anything could satisfy it, including myself.

"Open up for me," he instructs, grabbing my ass cheek with his free hand and spreading me apart. He fucks me harder. Violently. I groan, burying my face into the mattress and biting down on the bed sheets. I've never felt this consumed.

"More, Cora," he demands, slamming into me with no remorse. I accept it eagerly, whimpering at the incredible sensations.

"Fuck," I scream, grinding myself against whatever the hell is making me feel so good, whatever is far wider and deeper inside of me than any man or dildo has ever been.

My juices drip down my thighs, soaking the mattress beneath me as I cry out repeatedly, overtaken with pure adrenaline and euphoria. My senses become heightened. The scent of sex and sweat fills the air, along with the heady scent of Nolan's lingering cologne. My toes curl and my hands ball into tight fists at my sides. I inhale a long breath, claiming this inevitable orgasm and riding out every incredible second of it.

Unexpectedly, Nolan leans against me, his body pressed to my backside as he reaches around to grip my throat. I begin panting, before he clenches tight. Oxygen deprived, and now gasping for air, I push back against this invasion even faster.

"That a girl," he laughs savagely over my desperate cries, his lips brushing against my ear as he continues to fuck me mercilessly with the cold, hard object. "Take it," he grunts with each thrust, increasing his pace as he tightens his vice grip on my throat. "You have no fucking choice but to take it."

Hell, he's right. I don't have any choice. I'm bound. As helpless as one can be.

Except, if I did have a choice, I'd still choose *this*.

Him.

My pussy grips the object tight, holding it hostage as it moves within me. I clench my thighs together and my body trembles, wave after wave of a second—or third—climax ricocheting through me. I've never felt anything this powerful. Nobody has ever gotten me off like this. Or even at all.

He's a psychopath, in every sense of the word, yet he doesn't scare me one bit. In a world full of pitch-black-nothingness, he makes me feel alive. Like I am capable of anything.

Like the whole world is ours to own and to play with.

Our own bloody playground.

He releases my throat once he senses I've begun to come down from my high, withdraws the object, and flips me onto my back in one swift motion. And when my eyes set on what he's been using, my jaw drops.

It's a bone.

He's been fucking me with a bone this whole time.

And it's just given me the best fucking ride.

"Did—did you just—"

"I did," he cuts me off, staring down at me with those menacing eyes before inspecting it closely. "And all this cum, *your* cum, is proof you enjoyed it."

He smiles, *really* smiles, before delicately placing his new favorite toy back into a box. Then he retrieves his knife and begins cutting away at the plastic, starting at my pelvis, and slowly trailing upward.

A knot grows in the pit of my stomach as I stare up at his face, watching him closely as the knife lightly grazes along my skin.

Sensing my sudden discomfort and suspicion, his jaw tightens, and he freezes, immediately locking his eyes with mine.

"Ask," he orders, his voice low. "You have a question, so ask."

"The bone," I mutter. "It's human."

"Yes," he answers.

My heart hammers. No. It's can't possibly be—

"You're telling me you don't recognize him?" he taunts, proving my gnawing suspicion accurate. "I know his flesh is gone now, and that he's in pieces, but still. What kind of friend are you, Cora?"

"Jerri."

He finally cuts away the last of the plastic wrap and I push myself up from the bed, lunging for the knife. Instead of putting up a fight, he releases it, handing it to me. I hold it tight in my grasp, and dart forward, pressing the tip of the blade against his throat, threatening to puncture his skin.

Nolan looks down at me, his hands loosely down by his sides, his shoulders relaxed. Yet his sharp, chiseled jawline remains tight. He breathes slowly, watching me intently, as if trying to read my thoughts. I lower myself from my tip toes down to my heels, breathing hard and fast, trying to figure out why I'm suddenly feeling the way I am.

Trying to figure out how I could have been so furious just seconds ago, and now I'm raging with lust and total admiration.

"Cora," he whispers, lifting his hand.

I press the blade against his skin more firmly, in an attempt to show him I have the upper hand, drawing a small bead of blood just below his jaw.

He brushes his fingertips against my face, his touch gentle, and welcoming. Stepping closer, he leans into the knife, blood trickling down his neck, and a fire ignites in his eyes.

My legs quiver from the sight of blood staining his skin. We're now standing so close together I have to crane my neck to look up at his face. Temptation creeps on up me and my hand begins to shake, until he grips my wrist, keeping me steady. We let out deep, shallow breaths, gazing into each other's eyes as an uncontrollable urge overpowers us.

Suddenly, we become one.

He pulls down his pants, bends down and lifts me from the floor, lowering himself onto the bed with me on his lap. I straddle him, still holding the knife to his throat as he rubs the tip of his cock up and down my wet slit. My breathing has become erratic, and my thoughts are racing. I continue to look him in the eyes as I sink onto his length.

"Fuck," he growls, taking my ass in his hands and easing me up and down.

I try my best not to cut him open or kill him.

I try really, really hard... until I lose myself in a moment of bliss from the feeling of him throbbing inside me, and I lean forward, plunging the blade into his shoulder.

He groans out in discomfort, gripping my arm with bruising force. His eyes are wide, filled with a rage I've never seen before. I'm almost certain he intends on killing me now. Until he catches me by surprise, his lips curling into a smirk, and he grabs my wrist, urging me to go deeper.

I roll my hips, working him as I sink the blade into his flesh another inch. He lets out a choked groan, squeezing my wrist so tight I begin to lose feeling in my hand. Tightening my fingers around the hilt, I lean into his chest, applying more pressure to his fresh, bloodied wound. His cock swells inside of me, twitching with desire.

"Fuck," he breathes, his eyes rolling into the back of his head.

"Nolan," I moan, twisting the blade as he growls out in pain. "You're bleeding." His eyes darken, and he leans in, his lips mere inches from mine. "You're bleeding just for me."

Without thinking it through, I yank the blade out of his flesh, watching the blood spilling out, trickling down his bicep at an incredible speed. The sudden high I have is indescribable. I bounce on his cock, gripping his other shoulder with my free hand, my gaze entirely fixated on the warm, sticky liquid coating his skin. It's so beautiful.

Beads of sweat roll down my forehead and a wave of warmth surges through me. I'm so hot. So turned on. So alive. I wind back my arm, holding the knife above my head as I ride Nolan with excitement, sitting back fully, accepting every inch he has to offer.

But it's not enough.

Not now.

Not after the wonderful feeling of burying this knife inside him.

I lower my hand, the hilt firm in my grasp, my fingers now white and numb. The second I press the sharp tip against his abdomen, he catches my wrist and twists my arm around my back. I cry out, shrieking with discomfort as he pins my arm against my backside with such force I succumb, releasing the knife.

"Once isn't satisfying enough for you?" he snaps, his jaw twitching with anger.

I look him dead in the eyes. "Why do you get to have all the fun?"

He wraps his arms around me and flips me onto my back. Suddenly, he's fucking me hard, slamming into me again and again, his hips smacking against my pelvis, his breathing deep, the bulging muscles in his arms and shoulders flexing with each movement.

His arm is covered in blood, and it continues to bleed, beautiful red droplets splattering against me and the bedsheets. I breathe in the scent of copper and soak in the sight of blood smeared across our bodies. Before I can even make sense of it, I'm running my tongue along his bicep, licking the crimson, moaning loudly.

"Mm," I purr, getting a new rush as the metallic taste mingles with my saliva.

With that, Nolan empties himself inside me, staring into my eyes intensely. I study him, watching as his jaw clenches tight. His eyes turn to small slits, and I sink beneath his scrutiny.

This heated moment full of lust suddenly becomes intimate. Sensual. His arms that were just holding up just seconds ago give out. Suddenly, his body is pressed on mine. Our faces are so close—his lips are right there.

My gaze lowers, locking on those full, pink lips, and I begin to fantasize about how they would feel against my own.

He leans in closer, tilting his head, his breath fanning against my mouth with each exhale. I swallow hard and struggle to find words.

Words. What are words?

No man has ever seen me. He's the first, and I'm not sure how I feel about that.

My thoughts are erratic. The tension is so fucking high. My blood is pumping. Ears are ringing. There's a pull between us.

Still slightly hard, he moves within me, rocking back and forth, his pelvis creating friction against my clit. A soft moan escapes me. Sparks fly. The chemistry between us builds and builds. His body tenses against mine, and sinks into me with slow, gentle thrusts. My eyes meet his once more, and I grab the back of his neck, drawing him closer.

We inhale each other's harsh, uneven breaths, and it's suddenly a staring contest between us two mutual monsters. I ignore the warm, sticky substance against my palm as I brace his shoulder, pulling him to me, closing the small space between us.

He quickens his thrusts and grips me tight, grazing his hand up my neck until he's gripping my jaw. The pleasure solidifies into something so powerful, and so breathtaking, I can't stifle the cries that erupt from my chest. The wonderous sensation builds until it... explodes like a bomb.

The peak is even higher than I imagined, gripping me tight, and holding me there, in a paralyzing sensation of pleasure so strong, it's almost too much to bear. It's so thrilling, and so out of this world that it almost breaks me.

He comes inside of me once more, and from the sound of his sharp groans and bewildered gasps, I know this feeling has gotten a hold of him, too. Eventually, we find our way back down again. I feel jolts and shocks as he pulls out of me. He falls onto his back beside me. My skin still feels like it's on fire.

Here we are, trying to gain control of our breathing while lying beside one another, covered in blood, sweat, and arousal.

I utter the first thing that comes to mind. "I could have killed you."

He stares up at the ceiling, lost in his thoughts.

I roll onto my side and study his reaction.

"I could have killed you, Nolan," I repeat.

"No," he answers coolly, as a matter of fact.

"No?"

"You couldn't have killed me," he says. "You wouldn't have, and you're not going to."

He turns his head and meets my gaze, cupping the wound in his shoulder with his palm to gain control of the bleeding. I blink at him incredulously, watching his lips part, waiting for him to finish.

"You're not going to kill me, Cora," he reiterates. "Besides, you're going to need me for this."

"For what?"

He crookedly grins, his dark hair a disheveled mess, and his eyes wild and unhinged. "To live out your darkest little fantasies. You need me."

"I don't need anyone."

"You're sloppy."

"So, what?"

"We're going to fix that."

My heart leaps at his remark, as my eyes flutter shut, and I smile to myself. He wants to teach me. How romantic.

Chapter Nineteen

Nolan

There is a mountain of work to do.

The thought occurs to me as Cora sleeps against me, her head resting on my chest. As we breathe together, the top of her head rises and falls, each time brushing against my lips as I look down and ponder her.

My orderly room has been destroyed. Plastic and blood are strewn across the bed, more plastic is on the floor. It bothers me. I told her she was sloppy, but I've been just as bad.

We have only a precious few days before people start noticing the disappearances. Jerald was one thing; a flaky college student who might go fluttering off to music festivals.

Michael was another issue. And once the police begin searching, it won't be long until they connect him to his patients. To Cora.

To me.

She stirs slightly and her arm, draped possessively over my waist, pulls me tighter.

How far gone is she, really? Is she simply a broken girl, lashing out at the world and all the men who hurt her? What am I to her, really?

The big bad wolf, but *her* big bad wolf. Am I a weapon, to be aimed and then discarded?

The wound in my shoulder twinges, as if it wants to remind me of the danger she poses.

Kill her.

Right now? In my house? C'mon.

Let's be real, Noly-boy, that's not why. You want to fuck her again, don't you? Are you getting attached, buddy? Maybe you don't want the house of corpses. Maybe you want a house and three kids with the raging lunatic who looks good in a dress, hmmm?

I listen to my mind arguing with itself, twirling the problem over in its mental hands, examining it from each angle. Jerald, Cora, Michael.

There was truth there. I do want her again. I want to see how far she will go. How close to gone she really is. How deep the well of rage and sickness lurks inside her.

Just stick to the plan.

Pin it all on her.

Staring at the red dot in my painting, I watch as the crimson widens and engulfs my vision. I succumb to a delicious daydream, imagining breathless newscasters describing the trail of victims.

"Nolan Graves, the notorious serial killer known simply as 'Jawbone' because of his tendency to take the jaw of his victims, is currently wanted by police in multiple states. Authorities are coordinating with the FBI and implore that the public come forward with any information. His number of victims remains unknown, however more and more information comes to light each day..."

Cora awakens; I feel her eyelashes flutter against my skin, and after a moment I can tell she's staring up at my face while I gaze at the painting.

"What?" I ask.

"I want to know what is next."

I look down at her. "Depends on how far you want to go, little monster."

She doesn't like that. I regret it; I'm tired and sore. I really don't want to wrestle around with this girl as she tries to stab me to death.

Over a fucking pet name.

Instead, she sits up. "There was a moment, when we were together, I... wanted to kill you. The same thing happened with Michael. It's this... *rush* of rage, and hate, and pleasure and—" she catches herself, embarrassed at revealing this vulnerable side of herself.

I roll my eyes. "Cora, I have killed two people. I'm going to kill more. I ate Michael's liver. I bit into it, and it popped in my mouth." I shake my head. "Tell me what you're feeling."

She turns those hellish eyes on me. Either the comment about what I did to Michael, or the fact that I was willing to listen to her twisted fantasies, gives a quiet, steely confidence.

"Here's what I want," she says, and I listen to her. What she's saying is risky. Violent. More than a little insane.

It turns me on.

Cora

There's a seductive ambience in this red, dimly lit nightclub. Heads turn and all eyes are on me as I head for the bar, neon lights illuminating beneath the countertops. I sit on the stool and brush my bangs from my vision, eyeing the bartender before he heads my way.

His gaze roams down my body, starting with my dark eyeliner showcasing my eyes, and my dark red coated lips, then down to my full breasts nearly spilling out from my low-cut dress.

I wet my lips with the tip of my tongue at the beautiful image in my head. Cutting his throat. Spilling his guts out. The list goes on.

"What can I get you?" he asks over the blaring music and drunken chatter.

"Rum and cherry coke."

Slightly turning in my stool as I wait for my drink, I begin to scan the room. It's a Saturday night, so the club is packed. Adrenaline is high. The dance floor is so crowded people barely have room to move their arms. The atmosphere is electric, and the music moves everyone simultaneously like puppets on a string. The scent of sweat, beer, and cheap cologne fills the air.

They jump and sway drunkenly, slurring their words, having the night of their lives as if they are free and nobody is watching. But I am.

I'm watching more closely than I ever have before.

Except I'm picturing them without skin.

Suddenly, a strange, nagging feeling creeps up on me. I shut my eyes for a brief moment, tuning into the sounds of pointless conversation and laughter that blend in effortlessly with the melody and vibration of the music blasting through the speakers.

"Here you are," the bartender says from over my shoulder.

I place a ten-dollar bill onto the granite counter and take my drink in one hand, sipping slowly as I turn away. Once more I allow my gaze to take in my surroundings, exploring everyone intently, focusing on one person at a time. A tall, dark-haired man immediately catches my eyes from across the bar.

I stare at him blankly, not daring to look away for even a second.

His lips curl into a grin as he brings his tall glass of beer to his mouth, tossing back every drop. I blink at him, tilting my head to the side. I turn away, unimpressed. Uninterested.

When out of nowhere, that nagging feeling returns, settling somewhere deep in my gut. A subtle, yet taunting warning.

I become frozen in place; the rim of my glass pressed to my lips. Everyone becomes a blur, now moving in slow motion. Time seems to stop. A familiar presence lingers in the crowded, hazy room, and my body immediately reacts. My endorphins skyrocket. My shoulders become tense. My pulse goes from a slow, steady rhythm to nearly bursting out of my chest.

Suddenly, I happen to catch a glimpse of movement from the corner of my eye. I follow it, watching carefully as a tall figure glides through all the bodies in motion. The figure disappears. Searching for the eerie, familiar shadow in a heightened state of euphoria, my heart skips a beat, and my breathing hitches in the back of my throat.

Without warning, I find it.

Him.

Nolan.

And he's already staring.

As hot as it is in this club, a cold rush of air brushes against my skin. Our eyes lock in a stare so brutal, so intense, that I find myself completely breathless for the first time in my life. Nolan's eyes are like daggers, piercing straight through my soul. Everyone and everything fall away until he's the only person in the room.

Drawn to him like a magnet, I toss back the rest of my drink and set it onto the bar behind me. But when I turn back around, he's nowhere to be found. I hop down from my stool and rush toward the dance floor, weaving through everyone in search of the only person who has the power to make me *feel alive*, but he's gone.

Someone bumps into me, almost sending me flying backward from the force. I stumble on my heels and a pair of strong, masculine arms catch my fall. Letting out a soft gasp, I stare up into the glowing, menacing eyes of my dark-haired monster.

"Nolan," I breathe.

He brings me into his chest. There's a deep, powerful energetic exchange between us as he stares into my eyes.

He grabs the back of my neck and leans in, his hands slipping down my back, gripping my ass and squeezing, pressing me against him. A moan escapes my mouth, and that's when something breaks. Whatever pane of glass that was keeping us apart shatters entirely.

Suddenly his mouth is on mine, his tongue frantic and forceful in my mouth, my fingers tangled in his hair as his hands greedily roam every curve of my body. I've never had a first kiss feel anything like this.

A part of me wants to break away, and another part wants to never let go.

He traces the tip of his tongue along the scar on my lip, and fists my hair, tugging tight. We both pull away at the same time, staring at one another incredulously.

He blinks at me.

"I—"

"You ready?" he asks.

I nod.

Nolan

Cora breaks away from me and disappears into the mix of frothing people. The thudding music hurts my head, the haze of smoke, cologne and perfume gives the place the sickening reek of candle store.

My role in this is to hang back while she lures our victim. With that dress she's wearing, it shouldn't be a problem.

I order a drink at the bar and pay cash. The bartender, in a black tank top and jeans, smiles at me as he slides the beer over to me. "Where's your friend?" he calls out.

"Ex!" I yell back over the music. I pull down the neck of my shirt and turn so he can see the stab wound Cora left. "I need to leave her, she's crazy."

The bartender raises his eyebrows and quickly moves away.

When the police track our whereabouts, they'll interview him. And he'll say how he saw us together. That I was already worried. That I'd already been hurt by her. And when the police eventually arrest Cora, they'll think I'm one of her victims.

I see Cora across the room, pressing herself against a guy, running her hands down his chest. She's talking, saying anything that'll get him back to Michael's house with us. The guy is tall, decent looking, but wearing too many rings and a gaudy necklace. His silky red shirt is a bit too dressy for this place. He's trying too hard. He's probably wearing too much cologne. I wonder if he's coming off a bad breakup and looking to do something risky.

Cora nods over at me. I nod back.

So, we're really doing this.

What part of the house of corpses is this, Nolan?

Why, it's the weird sex part. Every serial killer has one. I need to fill out the Wikipedia page; the tawdry, sickening details that makes the people squeal and shudder.

They get back to Michael's house before I do. I pull the car in and sit in the driveway for a moment. The car smells like Michael. Whatever soap or cologne he uses is imprinted on the leather. It smells citrusy, like lime.

He didn't smell like this when I was cutting him open. He doesn't smell like this rotting in one of the empty train cars.

His car, his house, his smell... maybe I should've tried to wear his skin.

Another frantic, flashing fantasy bursts through, and I see myself wearing his face, stapling it to my own, layering it on my own skin, feeling it ripple and move with each breath.

Wearing it, then sprinting into Michael's house, a chainsaw roaring in my hands, gleefully driving it into the first person I came across. Cora, her new friend, it didn't matter. The tenuous grasp I had on rationality would dissolve away and I could go shrieking into hilarious madness. No more Nolan, no more fake smiles and pretending to be alive. Just the final crescendo of violence tearing everything apart.

A light clicks on in Michael's living room.

I have to go in there, and for a while, pretend to function. To coax the little psycho into her first kill.

But first, I have to talk a strange guy into a threesome with another man.

With *me.*

I burst out laughing, bitterly, because I'd rather cut off someone's face and kill a roomful of people than admit that this makes me nervous.

They're sitting on the couch when I walk into the room. Well, he is. Cora is pouring drinks. The guy smiles at me, starts to stand up, then sits back down, his smile widening.

"Sorry, I—do we shake hands?" he questions awkwardly. "I've never done this before."

Cora hands me a drink. I sip it and wince; she poured way too much bourbon in it.

"So, how should we get started?" she asks.

"Well, we should have a discussion first, I don't even know your name—" the guy stands up and tries to shake my hand again.

If this is how the night is going to be, I'm going to slit my own throat.

"Sit. Down," I tell Cora's friend, setting my drink down on the mantle.

I don't mean to be quite so threatening, but something in it makes him blanche and he stumbles back down, glancing at Cora for assurance. He's wondering if this is a mistake; he's wondering if Cora looks good enough for this to be worth it.

There is a twisting headache building in my temple that makes me slightly dizzy. I close my eyes, briefly, steadying myself.

"Look, if we aren't comfortable, it's no big deal—" he starts saying, but I'm already turning, grabbing Cora by the back of the neck and pushing her toward him, standing her in front of him as I pull down the straps of the dress.

"The only question," I say, sliding the dress down to her waist, "is what Cora wants."

She glares at me, our usual battle for control flaring again.

"So, what do you want, Cora? Do you want us to worship you? Treat you like a goddess?"

I begin kissing down her neck gently, working my way down to her bare shoulders. My hands move to pull her against me in a firm, loving grip. She is rigid for a moment, before melting in my arms, leaning her weight against me.

My grip tightens. My teeth sink into her shoulder, making her cry out. My hands stop their smooth embrace and clutch at her, gripping her throat.

"Or do you want us to treat you like a fucking toy?"

Cora reaches down and steps out of the dress completely. "Toys are more fun, don't you think?"

I have to give her credit; she knows how to play along. I drag her over to him and shove her to her knees at his feet.

"Alright, take it easy," he says, alarmed. His eyes flit down to Cora, then up to me.

"Take off your clothes," I tell him.

He frowns, but starts fumbling with his belt, licking his lips and staring at Cora as she slips between his legs and begins caressing his thighs.

"Okay, just, ease up, okay?"

I retreat back and sip my drink. "Do as you're told. Put your dick in her mouth. Now."

For a moment, I think he's going to get up and run. I would; every fiber of my being would be screaming that this is a trap.

But Cora is undeniable. She looks back at me with a naughty smile and leans forward, showing off her ass and bare pussy to me as she pulls his pants down, his cock springing free and wobbling in front of her. She grabs it and looks back at me again.

"You're not going to make me jealous," I say, swirling the bourbon and coke, trying to mix it better. "Now suck it. I'm getting bored."

She slowly takes him in her mouth, opening her jaw fully and letting him hit the back of her throat in one smooth motion, before pulling back and coating the tip in saliva. He groans, his hands balling into fists and hitting the couch cushions in pleasure.

"Hold onto the back of her head while you fuck her mouth."

He glances up at me. "I don't know if she'd like that—"

Cora releases him with a gasp. "Please, Ryan, I want it."

She starts stroking him furiously, her makeup smeared, her hair disheveled. I can't stop staring at her ass, but I catch the name.

"You heard her, Ryan. Be a good boy."

Tentatively, he grabs a loose handful of her hair and begins pumping his hips, his cock sliding in and out of Cora's mouth with wet sounds. Drool leaks between her lips; I see it getting on the carpet.

I finish the drink, then slowly slip off my clothes. Ryan keeps glancing at me; I get the sense that he's not very experienced and this is all very new to him. But he's been obedient so far, and I like that.

"With a toy," I say, grabbing the back of Cora's head and pulling her off of him, "you really get to take control of it. You don't have to care what it wants or how it feels."

I hook one of my thumbs on the bottom of her mouth, pulling it open. I can't read the expression on her face; it's somewhere between hostility and interest.

I kiss her forehead, and her eyes close.

Then I spit in her mouth; some of it hitting her chin in a glistening mist. I bring my hand down harshly on her ass and order, "Do not swallow." Calmly, I turn to Ryan. "Spit in her mouth."

He stands up and scratches his head, looking faintly ridiculous with his erection pointing at us like an exclamation mark. I lean forward and whisper in Cora's ear.

"If he says, 'I don't know, let's take it easy' one more time, I'm killing him, and you can't stop me."

To my surprise, Ryan knocks my hand away, taking Cora by the chin, brings his lips to the very edge of hers, and spits in it.

"Good. Now put your dick back in her mouth. And Cora?" I smack her ass again. "Suck it better this time. Like I know you can."

As I watch Ryan press his cock between her lips, I wonder if all this taunting will get me killed one of these days. Cora does have the capacity for violence, just a certain lack of follow through.

She crawls forward a bit and does a move I haven't seen from her yet, taking him as deep as she can and then shaking her head slowly back and forth while looking adoringly up at him.

"Oh my God," Ryan groans, and he tilts his head toward the ceiling.

That irritates me. I am hard, achingly aroused, but at this point it might be more in anticipation of watching her kill him. Every kill so far has been mine, an act of labor and effort. Might be nice to let her do all the work. Whatever Cora is doing with her mouth must be making Ryan weak in the knees, because he backs up and sits back down on the couch. Cora—*sexy* little Cora—keeps sucking the entire time, crawling to stay with it, her eyes never leaving his face. Her ass sways invitingly before me. I reach out and grab her hips, but she pulls away from me, glancing back at me and shaking her ass a little, grinning.

My hands spring out again and grab her ankles, dragging her backwards away from Ryan, sliding her on the floor on her stomach. Before she can raise herself, I bury my face in her ass, my hands pushing her thighs apart as I run the tip of my tongue from the very bottom of her folds, pressing firmly with my bottom lip and jaw, my neck stretching so I can get underneath her. I lick upward in one slow, forceful action, stopping and swirling my tongue in a luscious motion around the rim of her ass. I feel her tense up, and the taunting, vaguely amused tone she normally has slips as she lets out a low moan, followed by a demand through gritted teeth.

"Do that again, Nolan."

I do as I'm told, this time inching two of my fingers inside of her while I move my tongue faster, curling it into a U-shape as it slips deeper into her hole. I've never seen her so wet. I hear movement above me and glance up to see Ryan standing over us, stroking his cock and watching. I stop what I'm doing.

"No—please don't stop," Cora whines, and I gesture for him to grab her arms as I seize her legs.

"To the bedroom," I tell him. "We'll play with her there."

Together we twist her around on her back and lift her like she's a piece of furniture. Ryan walks backwards as she swings between us. She's facing me, watching me with interest. She bites her lip and lets out a small laugh, then says to me, "I think his dick is bigger than yours."

I smile back, picturing her in my shipping container, her stomach open before me with my fingers deep inside the wound, pulling out all her squishy, hot organs.

"You evil little slut. You want us to fuck you up, don't you?"

She sticks her tongue out at me. "You boys are all talk."

"You guys are insane," Ryan says. He's smiling too, we're all smiles, our happy little fuck-fest. I make a kissing face at Ryan.

"You have no idea, baby. No *fucking* idea."

Chapter Twenty

Cora

The mood changes when we get to the bedroom. The playfulness—or whatever Nolan's version of playfulness is—disappears, and it quickly becomes clear that he meant it when he said I was going to be their toy.

I'm thrown violently onto the bed. Before I can sit up and get my hair out of my face, one of them is on me, spreading my legs apart and sliding into me, pausing to straighten up on the bed before he begins thrusting in earnest, feverish strokes.

It feels good, and I like the way he holds one of my thighs with his left hand, hooking it between his bicep so I can feel it straining against my skin. I even like the way his hair is disheveled and the short, harsh breaths that feel hot against my breasts as he buries his face between them but...

It isn't Nolan.

My eyes find him as he crawls onto the bed beside me. He has that look on his face. That distant, vacant look; a plaster mask of inexpression. His mouth is frozen in a smirk, his eyes slightly narrowed. I wonder how long he's practiced this look.

There's a long scratch running a bright red line down the underside of his neck to his collarbone, and I reach up to caress it as Ryan grunts and thrusts even deeper into me, lifting my hips, making me let out a moan.

Nolan knocks my hand away.

"You don't get to touch me yet."

I start to roll my eyes, turning my head away from him but both of his large hands grab me, seizing my face and throat. There's a callus on his left palm; I can feel it on my throat, the rough abrasion rubbing against me.

I grab that wrist, and direct that hand downward. Nolan lets me, his expression slightly more interested, as I steer his palm down my body, over my breasts, his hand gripping each of them, the callus teasing my nipples in an achingly sweet twinge of nerves.

Ryan asks, "Do you like that, huh?"

"Shut the fuck up," Nolan orders. His eyes never leave my face, and I see the glint of homicidal fury that flares there. As if he just remembered Ryan exists; an alarm clock waking him from a pleasant dream.

Ryan falls silent and fucks me faster, the slight curve in his dick grazing my G-spot but not hitting exactly, making me more and more frustrated with each thrust. I need more.

Both of my hands on Nolan, I pull his between my legs, his finger spreading apart to let Ryan's dick keep sliding in and out of me. There's another pause; Ryan is unsure of having another man's hand so near him.

"We didn't tell you to stop," Nolan says.

The callus is right against my clit. I press his hand down and grind it against me, ecstasy exploding within me as Ryan picks his pace back up.

My orgasm is sharp, brief, and brilliant.

Nolan watches it all happen.

Then very quietly says, "Give her to me."

Ryan withdraws from me as Nolan rips one of the pillows off the bed, shaking the pillow out of the silky case and tossing it aside. Still holding the pillowcase, he tells me to bend over on the bed. I do as I'm told, confused, thrilled, and more than a little turned on.

Nolan throws the pillowcase over my head. Darkness envelopes me, sound is muffled, the fabric pressing harshly against my eyelashes. Each breath I take draws the cloth tighter against my mouth, wetting the fabric as I struggle for air. I feel him wrap it around my throat as he slides into me from behind. I am shoved down into the bed, as he savagely fucks me, a steady stream of insanity coming out of his mouth and into my ear as he pants and groans against me.

"You thought you were special, didn't you? You're just another toy, Cora."

His hands begin striking my ass, alternating between each cheek.

"All this bullshit about being crazy; about being like me..." His thrusts stop their rhythm, and he starts working in short, brief bursts, burying his dick as deep as he could inside of me, like he was using it to punctuate each word of his sentences.

"You're. Nothing. A tourist. A little brat who thinks she's more fucked up than she really is."

I gasp, caught between a building orgasm and confusion—was this part of the game, or are they his real thoughts? Why do I feel a twisting sense that I had to prove myself to him? I hate it... and fuck, I love it, too.

"Go get a knife from the kitchen," Nolan says. For a moment, I think he is talking to me, but then Ryan asks why. "To cut a hole in the pillowcase. You want her to keep sucking your dick, don't you?"

Nolan's voice drops and his grip loosens on me. I feel his breath in my ear, and his voice is earnest, excited.

"I'm going to leave the knife on the bed for you. When you want to kill him, tell him you want us to come on your face."

His breath leaves my side and I feel it on my back as he gingerly kisses down it with sweet, almost innocent kisses.

Sometimes he's shockingly tender, other times he's a fucking nightmare.

"Did you guys' spill wine or something in the kitchen? There's a stain." Ryan's voice wanders, bringing me out of my emotional turmoil.

"Yeah. Spilled a bunch," Nolan grunts. He pulls out of me, then tilts my chin up. "Hold still and open your mouth as wide as you can."

There's the sound of fabric ripping as he pokes the knife through, and suddenly something sharp and metallic on my tongue.

"Hold still," he warns again, rotating the knife and sawing away a rough circle. He removes the knife and tears away the rest. His thumb rests in my mouth for a moment, and I flick it with my tongue before biting down on his knuckle.

When he groans in a mixture of pleasure and surprised pain, a thrill shoots through me and I want him more than ever.

Something touches my hand beside me on the bed.

The knife.

Nolan is serving Ryan to me.

My last boyfriend didn't even get me flowers.

Someone gets onto the bed in front of me, and a dick is shoved rudely back into my mouth as Nolan slips back into me from behind, both of them pumping into me with savage lust.

This is fun, but it has gone on long enough. I grip Ryan's cock and stroke it, while blindly looking upwards, the pillowcase reducing everything to a muffled shadow.

"Take this off," I demand. "I want to look at you while you come on my face."

Nolan groans and I feel him release inside of me. He laughs a little, and I get the feeling it was the idea of me killing someone in front of him that made him finish more than anything else.

Ryan rips the pillowcase off my head, grinning down at me. My eyes adjust to the light again as my hand curls around the hilt of the knife. Nolan's hands are still around my waist, and he's still thrusting in and out of me gently, my pussy slick with his cum.

I smile sweetly at Ryan as he shuffles forward, his knees pressing deeply into the mattress.

"She's doing so good, isn't she?" Nolan asks.

Ryan loses focus on me, his eyes flicking up to Nolan's. He starts to say something, but the distraction is just long enough for me to raise myself, gain leverage, and bury the knife into him, just below his belly button and above his mound of pubic hair. I pull down, hard, the blade twisting against something—bone, maybe—carving a backwards J-shape into his crotch, the knife popping out as it scrapes against his penis and knicks the fleshy pouch of his testicles.

I swear Nolan gets hard inside of me again watching it happen.

Nolan

There's a small moment of stillness after she rips the knife out of him. A moment of post-sex relaxation fused with the time-slowing anticipation of the frenzy to come. I can hear my pulse in my ears. My mind is peaceful; blank. Like when you walk out of your house in very cold weather, the ice and cold of a freezing January morning seeming to suspend the entirety of existence and you don't even dare disrupt it.

My adrenaline starts to build. Cora is very warm on my cock, and I can hear her breathing heavily.

No blood comes from the wound at first.

The thing about killing is that it is oddly anesthetic sometimes. A mildly anti-climactic nature. Maybe movies and TV have ruined my perception, but a real kill…

There's always too much blood or not enough. Skin looks rubbery even when you cut it. It always feels like you're playing with dolls rather than hurting real, living creatures. I could slaughter the world and frolic in an ocean of blood, and I get the feeling it still wouldn't be deep enough for me to really dive.

The scene before me is picking up the pace. The blood is here now; thick, bright red and heavy as it spatters onto the comforter. Ryan seems to have found his voice.

"What? What?" is all he can say.

His left hand clutches his crotch, the blood spilling out between his fingers. His right jumps to his hair and grips it in a freakish, panicky motion.

Cora *thrusts* herself back onto me—I'm hard again, there's no fighting it—pressing her ass against me, raising the knife again.

I'm oddly proud of her.

Ryan shrieks, high-pitched and girly. He swipes his right hand across Cora's face, knocking her to the side. His fingernails run ragged scratches across her flesh.

He tumbles off the bed with an amusing thump, then retches, and gets up, knocking a bunch of stuff off Michael's dresser, before stumbling toward the door.

Cora stands up.

"Run, man!" I cheerfully cry after him. "She's crazy! We have to run!"

Following him down the hall, I excitedly join the sprint like it's a kid's race.

Ryan's face is now white, and his lips are a shade of purplish blue. "Help me, help me," he says in a strained voice.

"Yep, yep, let's get out of here," I tell him pleasantly.

When he gets to the kitchen, I stick my foot out and trip him.

He goes flying, skidding along the smooth tile floor, a streak of blood sloshing behind him. His collides with one of the cabinets, breaking the cheap painted wood and leaving a dent.

"Ryan, whaddya doin'? There are crazy naked people trying to kill you, get off the ground!"

He rolls onto his back and looks at me, incredulous, fighting the pain to realize I am just as eager as Cora is to watch him die.

He starts to crawl away, but I hold his leg down with my foot. He's very weak right now—whatever Cora hit with the knife must've been major.

She appears at my side like a ghost. There's blood down the front of her; her breasts are slick with it. She's ignoring me as I look her up and down, enjoying the chaotic view.

She leaps on Ryan, straddling him, holding him down with one hand, the muscles in her shoulders, back and thighs straining and flexing as she uses her entire body to pin him in place.

The knife makes such sweet noises as Cora drives it into him, over and over. A wet, punchy sound.

I wonder vaguely what it would be like to fuck Cora on top of Ryan's dead body, but I let that fantasy go the moment she starts doing snow angels on the floor in the bloody aftermath.

We have too much to do.

First, we must celebrate.

I join her on the kitchen floor, eyes fixed on the side of her face as she smiles widely, having a special moment all to herself. She appears proud. Like she has finally found her happy place, and for some odd reason, I find myself sharing these emotions with her.

Abruptly, she turns my way, locking her eyes with mine.

"I'm a murderer," she says, finally coming to grasp with reality.

"Indeed," I reply. "You *monster*. How *ever* will you sleep at night?"

A small grin plays at her mouth, yet she stays quiet.

"How do you feel?"

She glances down at her hands, at the knife she's still holding, trailing her gaze beside me to the limp form of Ryan crumpled on the floor.

"I feel incredible... alive..." She casually wipes the blood off the knife, rubbing it back and forth on the top of her thigh. Then her hand suddenly encircles my cock, grasping it tightly. "And like I need to be fucked again. Right now."

"We gotta get your boyfriend's body out of here. We have to clean up the house. We have a ton to do."

Hearing these words coming out of my mouth is dizzying. I sound like I'm fucking married. Next, I'll be telling her we need to get milk. Look at a brand-new washer and dryer. Bake a casserole for the neighbors.

She sits up and straddles my thighs, and I can't help but lock in on the knife. She's still holding it, that looming threat of violence lurking between us like a storm cloud ready to burst with rain and lightning.

It is uncomfortable to admit, but I am a little wary of her.

As soon as I start to sit upright, she pushes me back down, the knife point aimed at my bare stomach, Cora tracing circles in the air with it.

"How about we put the knife down?"

She laughs, and slowly runs the flat part of the blade along my sternum, before lifting my cock and rubbing the blade over the shaft, pressing it between her hand and the metal and moving it back and forth, the warmth of her palm contrasting with the coldness of the knife in a tantalizing way.

"Cora... what are you doing?"

"What?" she asks innocently.

We're in a pool of blood. So much blood. There's blood in her hair, and on her face. Blood on the floor. Blood on me. It's like the universe is serving me every pleasurable image it can, and it's setting off alarm bells.

Things are too good.

Cora takes the point of the knife and holds it to the underside of my erection, the point sharp and stinging... but not entirely unenjoyable. She edges it very slowly to the crease between where the head starts and shaft ends, letting the full weight of it rest there. Using just the knife point to hold it up, she sensually begins kissing the tip, her full lips enveloping it, her tongue wet and tortuous as she refuses to remove the knife, refuses to suck it fully. She simply teases me and watches me suffer.

"Oh fuck, Cora—" I don't have words anymore. I'm caught between agony and ecstasy.

"What? I'm just being your little monster." When her mouth forms the "r" sound, she bites down slightly, grazing me with her teeth. "I need you inside me again, Nolan."

She presses the head of my cock at her entrance and lowers herself onto me, taking me all the way. My hands find her hips, my fingertips digging into her skin. Cora's mouth falls open and her eyes roll into the back of her head, a tiny little cry escaping her chest. My cock swells as she rides me faster, rocking her hips, bouncing on my lap with a vengeance until she's begging me to come with her again.

That's when my cock erupts and I come harder than I ever have before, gripping her waist so tightly she grabs onto my wrists, crying out in pain.

My brain is in a pleasurable fog as I catch my breath, but one thought does manage to surface:

It is going to be really, really hard to kill her.

Chapter Twenty-One

Cora

Michael's shower, like the rest of his house, looks like no one has ever stepped foot in there. The gleaming tile makes our bloody footprints shockingly bright as Nolan ushers me into the shower and uses the extendable head to hose me off, spraying warm water up and down my body.

There's a moment afterwards where I'm worried that the mood will disintegrate. That we'll slip into some awkward small talk, a crazy, fake version of normalcy playing out while we stand in blood.

Almost desperately, I ask him to help me get rid of the body. I have a sense that there's a very brief window here in which I can ask more of him; I can ask him for anything with the way he's looking at me now.

I ask him to take me to the shipping container.

"Please, show me how."

He lathers some shampoo into his hair, ignoring me for a while. He is lost in his own world. What was it he said before? That killing made things quiet down for him? He seems to be enjoying that.

Over the sound of the water, he says, "Okay. I'll show you."

I smile. I can feel the trap I'm laying for him beginning to tighten.

Still quiet, still serene, he dollops a palmful of shampoo onto the top of my head, and then begins rubbing it in, massaging my roots with a calm smirk on his face.

Again, with the oddly caring gestures.

I guess it makes sense; how many people does he have some sort of connection to? Beyond manipulating them, beyond drifting between them and holding back violent urges?

The water on the floor of the shower flashes red as another splash of blood runs off our naked bodies. Then foamy soap mixes in as he rinses my hair out.

We stay in there for a long time, until the water starts to turn lukewarm. I turn to get out, and he embraces me, hugging me very tightly.

"Whichever way this ends," he says, "I just wanted to say thank you."

"For what?" I ask, bewildered.

His lips are on my neck as he speaks. "I would've been waiting for years. Waiting to lash out. Telling myself it was too soon. You set it all on fire. I appreciate that."

He snaps the water off. He gets out and hands me a towel.

"Now, let's get rid of the body, sweetheart."

Nolan

Everything is easier with an extra pair of hands.

Wrapping the body in one of the stained, bloody comforters is easier with someone holding the other corner of the fabric. Carrying the body to the car takes half the time. She even holds the door to the garage open with one foot while we drag Ryan down the steps.

When we get to the trainyard, she asks what I've been doing with the bodies.

Instead of going to the shipping container, I steer the car between a loose collection of rusted train cars, half-sunk into the soft earth. I get out of the car and click on a flashlight. It's almost five in the morning; the first soft glow of the sun is beginning to light the horizon, but it is still very dark.

The train car I want is black, with yellow, faded paint decorating the sides and the rolling metal door. From what I can tell, it used to haul for a chemical manufacturing plant.

I pull open the door and shine the light on the rows of metal barrels, waist high, lined up like obedient soldiers.

"They're empty," I tell Cora. "Well, mostly."

I lean down and pick up a metal rod and slide it under one of the barrel lids. I hand Cora the flashlight, and with a grunt, I pop the lid off.

There's about a foot of greenish-blue fluid in the barrel. I stare at it for a moment; it reminds me of the bottom of a well. I imagine tumbling into it. Sloshing around at the bottom as it expands and becomes inconceivably large. My fingers sliding off the smooth walls as I try to climb out.

"Michael is in one of these?" she asks.

I nod. "Third one back. On the right." I smile. "Jerri's in here too."

She doesn't say anything. A lot has gone on between us since I took her friend's life; I wonder if she's still sore about it.

We haul Ryan in, delicately climbing into the train car like he's a grand piano we're trying not to scratch. His knuckles drag on the floor in a way that my mind latches onto and keeps replaying.

His legs go in the barrel first. He slumps, his hips catching the side and he threatens to fall over, the comforter slipping off his face, revealing the anguished expression he died with.

I place both hands on his shoulders and shove down, his legs folding against the barrel sides. He's taller than Michael and Jerald; he won't fit in the barrel as easily. I push his head down and an arm pops out, drooping over the edge of the barrel.

I hold it with both hands and lean my entire weight against it. The elbow is flush against the metal rim. It takes three tries, but on third, the arm snaps. There's a loud, light *crick*, like when you crack your knuckles, and I'm able to bend it and squeeze it into the barrel.

I hear another barrel open behind me. A suffocating waft fills the train car.

Once, the power went out for a few days in the middle of the summer, and I had to help my dad empty it. The rotting eggs and spoiled lunchmeat were one thing; a sour, acrid smell that seemed to work its way into our nostrils underneath the face masks.

But the salad; a huge container of it from a fourth of July party, had turned black and gooey. *That* vegetable rot smell, that smell of decay, was what seemed to seep into the walls of the fridge and made us choke back vomit as we hurried to toss it into black garbage bags.

Now, Jerald smells like that.

While Cora is busy, I remove the small knife from my pocket and quickly hold up Ryan's hand. There, under the middle and ring fingers. A ragged bit of blood and skin. Cora's. I scrape his fingernails a bit, getting some of it on the blade, before carefully enclosing the knife in a bit of paper towel.

I will have to come back and take his jawbone out. Michaels too.

I've just been *so* busy.

I put the lid on, having to press it on the back of Ryan's head to get it to fit. Like when the garbage can is full, but you don't want to take it out, so you push everything down as hard as you can. The lid goes back on, and I stretch, feeling the soreness in my shoulders and back.

Cora is staring at her dead friend.

I go to her side and look in at him too.

His face is tilted up at us. The eyes are open—soupy, blank, and white. They remind me of poached eggs. I can see the nail still stuck in the mole and I suppress a laugh. There's a blackened slew of blood that coats the entire front of his body.

The bottom half of his face is gone.

Getting the jawbone out was difficult. It took a lot of cutting, a lot of prying. He died... well, I don't know exactly when. Sometime when I was playing with his body. He passed out after the nail to his balls.

Cora shoves the lid over him and storms out.

Quickly, I go to each barrel and open them, steeling myself against the stench of the rotting corpses. With careful precision, I take the knife out of my pocket and use the tip to press the bits of Cora's skin under Michael's fingernails.

I do the same to Jerald's, although his fingernails have taken on a waxy, flimsy texture.

Ryan, Michael, Jerald. All connected to Cora. All have her DNA on them. All have been seen with her recently.

There will be inconsistencies and issues with framing her. A shrewd detective will see through it.

But...

Almost half of all homicides are unsolved.

And they'll have a salacious, pretty young girl as a suspect.

Oh, the headlines.

That'll make careers.

"The Train Car Temptress"

"The Honeypot Slayer"

And I'll be the body they never found.

Chapter Twenty-Two

Cora

The adrenaline from earlier has faded completely. My muscles are aching and sluggish, and a heaviness drags at me. When you're a kid, you can fall asleep anywhere, in the back of cars, on the floor. I remember playing outside after a snowstorm, trudging around for hours until finally sprawling out on my back in soft snow, staring up at ice-blue skies, watching thin wispy clouds drift by. Exhaustion brought its own peace.

I want that now.

But I don't have a snow field. I have my dead therapist's car.

Hoisting myself up onto the hood, I lean back on it, stretching out as much as possible. It isn't great, but it'll do. The windshield is hard against the back of my head and the hood creaks and pops each time I move, but I'm so tired I don't care. At this point, it feels like my bed. I close my eyes and doze lightly, examining the events of the last week in my mind.

Jerald's body seemed to mark something, a certain point of no return. I had looked down at the ruined, bloated corpse of my friend and felt very little. A small ember of anger, and I knew I could blow on it, make it burn into a raging fire or...

I could let it go. Become more like Nolan.

This whole time, I had thought I was pissed off about him taking my friend away from me, when it had been much deeper than that. Before I met Nolan, I have always wanted to kill, but I didn't know how. I knew that it was looked down upon and I thought it was an urge I'd have to learn to live with forever, without ever being able to unleash that part of myself.

Yet, Nolan did it with such ease.

What does he have that I don't, and most importantly, how do I get it?

As if summoned by my thoughts, the metal door of the train car screeches open, and I hear his footsteps.

If he asks me what's wrong, I'll scream. If I have to hear another man take that tone with me, like I'm a toddler throwing a tantrum, I'll lose it. I'll just fucking lose it.

The car dips lower and I hear the hood clunk as Nolan climbs up next to me. I refuse to open my eyes, but I can tell he's watching me.

Something warm and leather that smells like Nolan is laid over me. His jacket.

Opening my eyes, I see him lying next to me, his hands behind his head, propping himself up slightly so he can watch the beginning pinpricks of light coming over the horizon. He yawns lazily.

"What a day, huh? Do you want to get breakfast?"

He's doing it again. Being oddly sweet. The back and forth continues; one second showing you the body of your dead friend, and the next giving you his jacket and asking you to breakfast.

I can't take it anymore. I need clarity. Or confrontation. If he's going to kill me, fine. Fuck it, do it now. If he's going to say he loves me and wants to run away together, okay, sure, let's do that. I can't exist in the grey area between us anymore.

"Why do you do that?" I blurt out.

He turns slightly. "Breakfast? I'm a big waffles guy."

"No. You know what I mean. You kill people—"

"We both kill people now."

"And it's like you're plotting to kill me, then you're taking care of me instead. Sometimes you're nice, and sometimes you're pure fucking evil. You help me kill Michael, which, in your brain, was probably something really special, and then you hug me and thank me. Now you show me Jerald's corpse like you're proud of it. What..."

All the thoughts are spilling out of me, and I have to gulp the chilly air for breath. I turn on my side, nestling in his jacket even as I confront him.

"Nolan, what do you want from me? For this one moment, please, no schemes, no serial killer act. Tell me exactly what's on your mind. Do you have feelings for me? Do you even have emotions? What..."

My words trail off once again. I have gathered every conflicting idea in my head, wrapped them in question marks and hurled them at him. I half-expect him to simply get up and walk away.

"What am I thinking?" he muses. "Breakfast. I was serious about that."

I'm going to kill him. That's it.

He reads the look on my face and bursts into laughter.

"Yeah, yeah, I know what you mean." He scratches at the shadow of beard starting to grow along his jaw as the smile fades. "It's weird; I have emotions. I can feel them, but they're muted. The volume on them is turned way down and they're very, very far away."

He reaches his hand out in front of him, mimicking grabbing something out of the air.

"The only way I feel emotion is if I chose to. Does that make sense? Things will happen and I have to manually decide; am I going to feel this, or not? And if I do, it's like I have to coax it into cooperating. After a while—" He shrugs. "—I stopped choosing. I got very used to that distant feeling."

"Why did you stop?"

"I didn't mean to. Now I'm this. That's the only way I know how to explain it."

Nolan grins as the sun begins to beam on us, closing his eyes and tilting his chin upward, relishing the warmth.

"I never wanted to exist, really. I was placed on this earth and told to walk around and learn these things and go to school and work a job and find a wife and do this and do that... and I never saw the point."

I move closer to him, our shoulders now touching. Every time he speaks it's as if he's taking paragraphs of tangled, racing thoughts out of my own head, reading the etchings off the inside of my skull.

"I thought I could hide with Natalie. I thought I was so good at pretending that I could slip amongst all those people who seem to know how to be alive and exist among them but—" His tone shifts, and he sounds almost bitter. "I would've let them carve out this part of me. Snuff it out so I could go to barbecue's and listen to Natalie talk about work."

I nod. "Then Cora comes along and ruins all of that."

His arm curls around me and pulls me very close, so that I can feel his chest rise and fall as he breathes.

"Yes. Yes, you did."

It's a nice moment. I can choose to accept it and enjoy it, or I can opt out and ignore it. I want to lean into Nolan and give up fighting. It's every girl's dream to be swept away by the blood and chaos.

I slide a hand across his stomach and cling to his hip, enjoying the warmth of him and the way he shifts to curve his body around mine. This is the part where something breaks. There can't be days like this, of coziness and comfort. Not for me.

Not with Nolan.

Right?

There's an urge to push this toxic relationship off a cliff; to dump lighter fluid all over something already burning.

We haven't spoken in minutes, a tender silence that could preoccupy me forever if I didn't want to ruin it.

"Nolan?"

"Hmm?"

"Do you have fantasies?"

He doesn't stumble over his words or try to get me to explain further to buy him time to think of something to say to me. Nolan nods. "Yes."

"Like what?"

"The usual. Threesomes. Wearing someone's face and seeing if I can pass for them for an entire day. Fuck their wife and rip the mask off at the last second and just... scream." He rolls on the hood of the car, facing me directly. "People ask questions like that because they want to talk about something. So, let's hear it."

"Clowns."

"Clowns." He reaches out and squeezes my nose. "Honk honk."

I slap his hand away, just for him to catch my fingers in his and reel me in, until my head is firmly underneath his chin and he's running his hand down my back.

"You want to paint your face and kill someone, don't you?" he murmurs.

I nod against his chest.

My heart is pounding but his pulse doesn't change. His heartbeat is a solemn drum against my ear.

"My parents took me to a circus when I was little," I begin, "and there were these clowns. They had their stupid faces painted and they bothered me so much. I remember everyone in the crowd laughing hysterically. I wanted to laugh, too, but I couldn't. I didn't understand what the point was. Their outfits and the overly exaggerated face paint felt like an inside joke that everyone was a part of except for me."

Nolan stares at me silently.

"The only joke... is life. Life is one big fucking joke," I explain. "So, I want to dress like a clown next time around. Give it a whirl." My smile fades. "But this time, I wonder if they will be laughing when I'm standing over their bed with an axe."

"Interesting," he breathes, tracing the back of my hand with his thumb. "There's a new movie playing at the theater."

"Oh? What's it about?"

"A man dressed as a clown, cutting apart all the filthy young people who dare to have sex."

I arch a brow at him. "Is this your way of asking me out on a date?"

"Maybe."

He's quiet, thinking to himself for a long time, so long that I get ready to dismiss the thought all together.

"Cora," he speaks up, twirling a lock of my hair around his finger while his eyes bore into mine. "Will you go out with me?"

Fighting a grin on my lips, I return my gaze to the sky. "Sure."

Nolan

Cora might tell herself she's a monster. Fangs and all, sure.

But really, she's easier than Natalie.

Just another bright-eyed girl desperately needing someone to pet her head and tell her I accept her. Natalie might have self-esteem issues and the aching need to please someone, but you can palette swap them. Red lipstick for black. Cora needs someone to tell her that the murder and blood fantasies are fine.

Sweetheart, of course they are.

But she's a Halloween store. Smoke and mirrors, rubber knives and face paint. She wants to play "killers" and wear the mask but really, would she be here without me?

I'm the vicarious thrill. Girls want bikers, rockstars, or vampires.

Some want serial killers.

Monsters that can take them on dates and echo civility. Monsters that'll take them to the movies and hold their hand when the jump scare happens.

We're too early for the movie. A litany of sneak previews flicker before us as we settle into the half-full theater. Cora clutches a bucket of popcorn that's bigger than her head.

Our squashy reclining seats engulf us. More people file in.

Groups of people lose details to me almost immediately; they become faceless mimics of each other. This smudge.

Test her.

The thought swims into focus and I regard it with amusement. What would test her? I'm certain I can talk her into almost anything.

Give her a Nolan fantasy.

I nudge her. "Clowns are your fantasy. Would you like to hear another one of mine?"

"Does it involve that thing you do with your tongue?"

"It can. My first fantasy, the first dream of killing someone, I had this idea about phone books."

"Phone books," she echoes dryly. "Nobody uses those anymore."

I give her a look. "They would get delivered to our door. A yellow and white paged book full of numbers and locations. I wanted to pick a random address out of the book and kill everyone in the house, leaving behind the page with their name and number circled. Tack it to the wall with the remains of their face pinned next to it, dripping like a fried egg slapped onto a plate."

On screen, an actress talks about her upcoming movie. A couple sits down; a person with black hair sitting next to one with brown hair. Both are wearing denim, which bothers me.

The lights darken, and we're coated in a smooth, soothing blackness. Cora crawls over and sits on my lap, leaning back against my chest, her cheek flush against mine. She takes my hands and pulls them around herself like a warm blanket. "Tell me what you want to do, baby."

Why does she smell so good?

I squeeze her tighter. "Of all the days, of all the people to come across, they came across me, because I just so happened to lay my finger on a number in a book."

The movie starts. The opening scene features a grotesque clown dragging a body in trash bag down a dark road.

Cora guides my hands between her legs, closing her thighs around them and making me feel how wet she is. Then she takes my left hand, daintily extends a finger, and begins aiming it around the movie theater.

"Eenie," she says, aiming it one corner, at a group of three young men, guffawing and tossing popcorn at each other.

"Meenie," she continues, pointing at an old couple in the front, the light of the screen reflecting off their glasses.

"Miney." She hits a lone person with red hair, and Cora begins grinding her hips against me, and I have to bite her shoulder to keep quiet.

"Mo."

It's the couple in denim, but I don't really care. I want to shove Cora on the ground and fuck her brains out.

"Catch a tiger by his toe. If he hollers let him go. Eenie, meenie, miney, *mo*." She moans the last word into my ear, biting my earlobe and pulling on it lightly with her teeth.

"Them? Tonight?"

"Mmhmm."

"We follow them home, we get their address, then we come back in face paint and kill them in their beds."

Cora sighs with pleasure. "I love it when you talk like that."

There's a clown chasing someone down with a chainsaw. Cora watches it and pulls my arms around her, nuzzling into me. The denim couple glances back at us. The woman frowns.

The man glares at me.

"Can I kill him?" I whisper to Cora.

"If you're a good boy," she whispers back.

Chapter Twenty-Three

Nolan

On my fourth date with Natalie, we went grocery shopping.

Yeah.

Somewhere in the barrage of text messages, she mentioned a thing she read that a good way of seeing if someone is compatible with you is to see how you like them in a mundane environment; one of those routine life tasks that you will ultimately be sharing thousands of with them over the course of a relationship.

"*Or a marriage. Ha ha, just kidding, lol,*" was her follow-up text.

We strolled among cans of soup, dodging shopping carts steered by old women and gum-chomping power dads determined to be the absolute best at shopping smart and Getting Deals™. She had a paper list detailing some pasta recipe, and took forever meandering around, looking at all the colorful products like a child gawking at the giraffes in a zoo.

I couldn't handle it.

I was having one of those lethal days where the air makes my skin itch. The lights are too bright; colors seem harsh on my eyes. There's a smell that seems to leak off of people; human existence, soap and sweat and all the desperation of being alive.

Plucking the list from her grasp I led her through the store, throwing the items into the cart without saying a word to her.

Later, in the car home, she asked what that was all about.

"Sorry," I said. "I just really hate grocery stores."

"*Thank* you! They're the worst! The aisles are too small! Why do they put the milk in the *back* of the store? And they never hire enough cashiers, so there's always a line. I *hate* grocery shopping."

She reached over and squeezed my thigh. "It was very hot the way you took the list from me."

I liked Natalie a little bit that day. Even if it was just the pleasant afterglow of hating something together. She wouldn't understand the urge to tear my own face off and scream in the middle of Aisle 9, but relationships were built on compromise, right?

Cora is...

Well, something else entirely.

I haven't bought her flowers or had to go grocery shopping or to a farmer's market with her. I haven't had to smile giddily as she hands me a cup of foul-smelling tea, listening to how "it's so much better than coffee, right?"

The face paint is irritating, though.

She becomes excited, sitting on the counter of Michael's bathroom and smearing paint on my face with her fingers. Blackening my eyes, she cakes it onto my eyelids which in return makes it difficult to blink. She draws a lopsided clown smile in white around my mouth, grinning at me before sticking her paint covered finger in my mouth, and laughing when I spit the paint back at her.

It's the first time I have seen her loosen up and smile; the strained, tight expression on her face dropping and revealing someone who could laugh and joke around.

That's when it hits me.

I am making her… happy.

When it's time for me to paint her face, I grip the back of her head and paint rough, jester lines vertically through her eyebrows and down her cheeks, then apply red to her nose. I end up giving her a droopy, sad frown in black and white, before painting spirals to the sides of her face.

"We should dye our hair," she exclaims. "Green? Purple?"

"Cora, we're going to spend longer getting ready than we are killing these people."

"Ohhh, I'm Nolan," she mocks, "I don't like anything! I just want to wrap people in plastic and eat them."

"Knock it off."

"Make me."

Gripping her thigh roughly, I lean forward, my lips nearly brushing hers. "We do not have time. If you want to do this, then we need to focus."

"We followed them home from the movies. We know where they live. We have a plan. We're fine."

"Cora," I snap, eyes wide.

She huffs. "Fine." Her smile broadens, working against the clown dismay I've painted on her. "Let's go to the garage. I want to pick out a weapon."

Now, I'm lurking in a car, face painted up as Cora seethes beside me.

We've combined two fantasies. Finding a couple by chance at the theater, wrong place, wrong time. Just like picking a random name out of a phone book.

Cora's is simpler, more direct. Smeared in clown makeup and terrifying someone before killing them.

Hot.

A little theatrical but fine.

It was easy to find their names after a quick Google search of their address. They're the type to review local restaurants. Lorrie Parker has lots of opinions on dessert options at "Sweet Eats Cheesecakes" and Colton Parker is "in love" with the craft beer at "Battered and Brews."

Most of my reasons for killing people are arbitrary. But we'll be doing the world a service by butchering the woman who left a one-star review at a medical clinic because "my nurse had way too many tattoos to be professional."

The Parker residence had lights on at ten o'clock, but by eleven thirty they were out. The house looms dark before us, and Cora begins to open her door. She's gripping a small hand axe she found somewhere in Michael's garage, and I eye it warily.

"Stay in the car," I order.

"No, let's go. They're asleep."

I extend my arm across her chest like I'm braking hard at a stoplight. For a moment, there's a feral, venomous look on her face and I worry she's about to bite me. "Calm. Down. Give them time to fall asleep."

She closes the door with a feral growl and settles back into her seat. The skirt she's wearing has ridden up around her hips and I can't help but stare. She makes no move to fix it, and instead glares out of the windshield, ignoring me.

She's bored, I can tell.

My hand is still across her chest but now I lower it to her lap. She glances at me, waiting to see what I'll do next.

"Spread your legs."

"I thought we were waiting until we got inside—"

Stop talking. Do as you're told."

She clicks her tongue but does it, lifting her knee over the center console and propping herself up higher in the seat. "What, now you're going to finger me like we're in high school?"

My hand drifts down and begins rubbing the fabric of the thin purple panties she's wearing. She groans and shifts her hips, holding onto my forearm, the axe still clutched in her hand. The blade is turned slightly and digs into my skin, but I don't mind.

"Tell me what you're going to do to them, Cora."

"What?" she breathes, flustered.

My hand begins moving faster. "Tell me how you're going to kill them."

"Jesus... okay... I'm going to... I want you to tie them to the bed."

"Yeah? Good girl, keep going."

"Then I want you to pull the man's eyelids back, waking him up as I stuff a rag into his mouth so he can't make a sound."

I use my fingers to nudge her panties to the side, the seam of the fabric brushing against her clit. Her hand turns into a fist as she drops the axe and punches the side of the car door.

"I'll be the first thing he sees. I'll see the fear hit his eyes as he realizes what I am. What *we* are."

"What are we, Cora?" My hand curls around her pussy, working slowly back and forth in short, horizontal bursts.

"We're a nightmare."

My dick grows in my pants as I laugh. "A little bit. How are we going to kill them?"

"Nolan," she whimpers. "Move your hand faster, please."

"Nope. Not until you tell me how you're going to kill him."

Her eyes flutter shut, and she tosses her head back in frustration. My fingers are slick with her arousal. I want to taste her, but I refrain. "I'm going to stand over his wife on the bed. I'm going to take the axe and—"

I move my hand sharply, like I'm swiping paper off a desk and her words dissolve into a moan. Her legs try to close around my hand. "Keep your fucking legs open and finish your sentence."

"I'm going to chop off the bitch's head! Then I'm going to bury this blade in her husband's fucking skull! Is that what you want to hear? I'm going to see if I can hit the spot between his eyes. I want to watch it split. I want to see if it's like the movies! I want to see what his mouth does as he tries to comprehend what I've done to him."

I spit on my palm and return it to her clit, rubbing it in while sinking two fingers inside her. She groans, grinding against me. "That's one victim, little killer. What should we do with the next?"

She turns to me, her eyes wide in the clown makeup. "I want you to fuck me on top of their headless bodies."

It's my turn to moan, my erection straining against the grey sweatpants I'm wearing. Her hand sneaks over and grabs it, pinching the fabric around it. "What's the matter?" she taunts. "Did you think you were the only one with nasty thoughts?"

It's midnight. The Parkers are respectable people with good office jobs. They have to be awake early in the morning.

They must be asleep. And I can't wait anymore.

We get out of the car, our heinous reflections glinting off the car as we are dimly illuminated by distant streetlights.

Cora takes my hand. I have rope. She has the axe.

Together, we walk toward the Parker house, ready to paint the walls in blood.

Cora

Nolan finds a seam in the sliding windows and manages to wedge his fingers in between the glass and the window frame. He pops it out, and silently shifts the pane of glass to the side, letting me climb into the house first.

We're standing in a dimly lit kitchen; a granite countertop sits in the middle of glossy tiled floors, and the gleaming stainless-steel appliances. It smells of lemon scented kitchen cleaner.

A thought crosses my mind. I wonder if the Parker's have ever fucked on this kitchen floor.

Striding quickly through the house in a murderous haze, I head toward the stairs until Nolan's hand catches my wrist.

"What?"

"Slow down," he hisses. "I can hear your footsteps."

"Are we going to kill them or not?"

His hand covers my mouth and I'm shoved against the wall. A hanging photo of the Parkers at a bar, raising glasses to the camera, shudders beside us but doesn't fall.

"I am not getting caught because of you," he murmurs. "You don't know what these people have. They could have a panic button that alerts the police of a break-in. They could have a gun, and I'll be collecting your guts off the ground because you couldn't keep yourself in check."

My hand snakes down and grabs his cock through his pants. He's still hard and becoming even harder beneath my touch. I twist my head around, freeing my mouth from his grasp. "Still want me to stop?"

"Just... slow down."

"Slow down?" I question, creating more friction as I rub him faster. "Are you sure?"

He groans. I let go abruptly and begin walking through the house. There's a spacious living room that has shelves full of action figures and collectible toys. There's a vintage sewing machine in the corner and one of those cube sofas that are made to be disassembled and rearranged.

Nolan trails behind me. He makes his way to the action figures, and gazes at them, before touching one of their upraised little swords. He paces around, looking at the framed movie posters and coffee table carved out of wood into the shape of a Star Wars spaceship. "I'm so glad we're killing these people," he whispers.

"Why?"

"Nerds. Stop.... buying things. It bothers me. Collecting plastic."

"You collect jawbones," I shoot back, catching a glimpse of something resting on the end table. After examining it, I let out a small giggle.

"What?" he asks, tearing it from my grasp and looking it over briefly. "Looks like they're behind on their mortgage."

I find the stairs. "Guess we're doing them a favor."

Halfway up, he snakes his arms around my waist and pulls me down, spinning me around and laying me on the carpeted stairs. The axe thumps quietly, and we both pause, listening for footsteps or muffled voices.

Nothing.

Although I don't think that would stop Nolan from shoving my skirt up and moving my panties aside again, his mouth wet and warm as he outlines my pussy with his tongue. I run my fingers through his dark hair while his gloved hands curl around my thighs, holding me firmly against his face. He groans, his erection jutting against his sweatpants.

My breathing hitches as a beautiful sensation begins to bubble in my stomach, until he looks up at me, smirking.

"Stay quiet, killer. Don't get us caught."

"You're the one groaning because you get to taste me," I counter.

He kisses the inside of my leg and then climbs past me, like we're racing up the stairs.

"Stop edging me," I snarl.

On the landing, he looks left and then right, before extending a hand and helping me to my feet. "Their bedroom is at the end of the hall."

We approach it like giddy children trying to sneak downstairs for Christmas presents. The door is shut, the only sound in the house a gentle ticking coming from downstairs and the whir of a fan from inside the room.

Nolan grabs the door handle, but before he can open it, I push him against the frame, pressing my lips to his. I kiss him deeply, my hands around his waist as he drapes his arms over my shoulders and returns the kiss. What was once a simple peck has become a passionate exchange of... emotions?

My heart swells and the blood swishes in my ears. The moment his hand lightly cups my cheek, I pull away frantically, his arm falling to his side.

"Tie them down," I whisper.

"I know, I know, shut the fuck up."

I'm finding that Nolan alternates between affection and annoyance quickly and easily; sometimes he has a shocking warmth and other times he's the biggest douchebag in the world.

But he's here, dressed in face paint, willing to kill for me.

The Parker's are curled around each other. She has her husband's head cradled against her chest, and her hands buried in his curly hair as he clings to her like a little boy. The blankets are intertwined and tangled together. They clearly need a bigger bed; it looks like they're sleeping on a queen. All their money went to knick-knacks and a dishwasher.

We are as quiet as a mouse. Nolan tosses the rope over them and has me kick the ends back under the bed so he can reach under and grab it. We do this several times, the red and black rope casting shadows over the passed-out couple. They sleep so peacefully.

He begins tightening the rope. Four strands, laid horizontally across their bodies. One at their ankles, one at their waist, one near their chest, and one for their throats. Nolan gathers the ropes in his hands.

"When I start tightening this," he whispers, his eyes gleaming orbs of light against the dark face paint, "they might wake up. Be ready."

"Yes, Daddy."

He closes his eyes and takes a deep breath, fighting back his irritation with me.

The joy it brings me to get under his skin... it's so rewarding.

Abruptly he begins tightening the rope. Pulling it, drawing it tighter and tighter, the rough edges of it rasping against the soft cotton of the Parker's baby blue bed sheets. The rope is a boa constrictor, tightening around an innocent deer, ready to devour it.

The woman awakens when the rope digs into her throat. She says something to Colton, her voice thick with sleep, and he mumbles back, "Sleep paralysis. S'okay Lorie."

Lorie tries to sit up, but can't, then strains against the rope. Nolan works faster, placing one boot on the edge of the bed and straining the rope as tightly as he can.

"Colton," she panics, trying to wake her oblivious husband until I retrieve a rag from my pocket and stuff it into her mouth. Lorie squirms against the ropes and screams into the fabric, except her cries are muffled and useless.

I turn on the light at their bedside table and stare down at Colton, waiting for him to awake from his deep slumber. He lets out a loud snore, slipping even deeper into unconsciousness.

"Yikes," I mutter.

Glancing over at Nolan briefly, I see him shrug, then my gaze settles back on the horrified expression plastered across Lorie's face.

"*Big* yikes. You married a fucking idiot," I taunt, resting the axe over my shoulder. "He's supposed to protect you. I bet you're wishing you could take back those marriage vows and call a do over right about now. Huh?"

Nolan's presence lingers behind me for a moment until he stands at my side.

"He's a big drinker, isn't he, Lorie?"

"Cora," Nolan urges impatiently.

"Okay, okay. Colton," I sing excitedly, leaping onto the bed while Nolan peels his eyelids back, exposing him to the dim light.

Finally, he comes to, Lorie struggles beside him on the bed, and a look of pure terror crosses his eyes. "Mm, what—who are—how—Lorie? Fucking Christ—" he blurts out, unable to form a single coherent sentence.

Rolling my eyes, I reach into Nolan's pocket and then shove the dirty rag into Colton's big yapper.

Yap-yap-yap.

"Look at us!" I exclaim, extending my arm and gesturing the axe back and forth between Nolan and I. "Don't we look great?"

The second I begin jumping up and down on the bed, a hot ache settles between my thighs. My nipples pucker at the image of slaughtering them in my head. Suddenly, I stop jumping and straddle Lorie's waist, caressing her face with my fingertips. "Listen, Lorie, we tried to be normal. Well, kind of. We went to the movies. You see, it was our first official date. I've never been on a real date before. Just Tinder hookups. Nolan and I had popcorn, and got to watch all the blood and gore on the big screen." I pinch her cheeks together and watch as tears cascade down her jaw and neck. "Except it wasn't enough. We couldn't feel the warm sticky crimson on our hands. Couldn't smell the strong scent of copper overwhelming our senses. Couldn't watch the *true* expression of life vanishing from someone's eyes."

Nolan groans.

I sigh dramatically. "Because at the end of the day, it was just acting. It wasn't real. But this?" I stumble back to my feet and grip the handle of the axe with both hands, raising it high above my head. "*This* is real!"

The axe swishes through the air and comes down hard on the pillow just beside her head. I missed.

"Whoops," I casually let out, before lifting my arms over my head once more and giving it another shot.

With perfect precision, the blade comes down and tears right into her throat, blood squirting out from her carotid artery in beautiful bursts. I swing again and again, cutting through flesh and bone, painting the walls the most glorious shade of dark red.

There's a light stirring of sensations building inside me with each passing second. Blow after blow takes me closer and closer. Higher and higher.

My limbs grow heavy. The sheets have become saturated with Colton's urine. He's screaming and crying. I lose myself in the chaos entirely. I'm covered in Lorie's blood. Nolan and Colton are, too.

Nine blows to the neck are what it takes to sever her head from her lifeless body. My endorphins are sky high, my thighs are slick, and my pulse is raging at the gruesome scene that has unfolded before my eyes.

Right on cue, after being edged by Nolan all night, an inevitable orgasm rips through my body. The peak is more intense than I ever could have imagined. I'm so far gone, lost in the pleasure of murder and lust. I'm not sure I will ever find my way back down.

I completely shatter, falling apart at the seams as I drop to my knees and release my grip on the bloodied axe. Thrashing forward, I cry out in bliss, gasping for air.

"Fuck," Nolan growls viciously, fighting back primal urges.

Clutching the bed sheets, I open my eyes, riding out the final wave of my climax as it carries me out to sea.

"Cunt!" a man's voice calls out. Colton has somehow managed to work the rag out of his mouth. "Crazy *cunt*!"

"What the fuck did you just call her?" Nolan demands. Suddenly he's taking the axe in a firm grasp and stands over him on the bed. "What the fuck did you just say to her?" The axe swings through the air before splitting his skull open. It's unlike any sound I've ever heard before. As eerie as it is, it's music to my ears. "Call her a cunt—" he grits out, "One." *Clunk.* "More." *Thunk.* "Fucking." *Clunk. Thunk.* "Time."

Colton's blood and brain matter spatters against my face with each blow. Nolan's face is red, and he is drenched in sweat. I have never seen him this angry before, and it's sending another orgasm through my body.

He turns to me, axe in hand, and eyes sinister. His chest rises and falls with each sharp, uneven breath. He's the most beautiful thing I've ever seen in my life, wiping the blood and sweat from his eyes with his forearm—smearing the clown makeup in the process—and watching my second orgasm rake itself through me.

Within seconds, he drops the axe to the floor with a loud thud before tossing me onto my back over Colton's dead body. Settling between my legs, he pulls out his hard cock and slips my skirt up my waist, staring into my eyes with violent bliss. As soon as he spreads my thighs with his knee, his hand locks around my throat and his mouth smashes against mine.

My face fills with heat. I can hardly breathe as he pins me down and slams inside me mercilessly. I scream out, bucking against his hips, grinding my pussy on his pelvis while he takes me with a vengeance. He increases his pace, thrusting into me hard and fast with no end in sight.

Clawing at his back, I bite down on his lip, drawing blood and sucking it into my mouth. The groan that escapes from his chest sends me spiraling.

He breaks our kiss, squeezing my throat. "Give me another one," he orders, my pussy throbbing and clenching tighter around his cock with each stroke. "One more, Cora," he harshly demands.

I release hoarse whimpers from my next impending orgasm, until he tightens his grasp once more, cutting off all air entirely.

My heart pounds. A rush of adrenaline courses through my veins once my body slips into a fight for survival. There's such beauty and peace that comes with fearful panic. Little black dots disrupt my vision before my eyes roll into the back of my head. Slipping further and further away, suddenly, I fall apart beneath him.

I come hard.

Harder than I ever have before. A release so powerful it's almost painful.

Nolan releases his vice grip on my throat and slams his fist into the mattress beside my head, keeping himself upright as he slams his hips against mine over and over, rocking my body back and forth on top of our lifeless friend.

With that, Colton's decapitated head rolls off the bed and collides with the floor.

"Cora," he breathes beside my ear, spilling himself inside me with sharp, urgent thrusts. "*Cora?*"

"Nolan," I whisper, tracing the muscles in his shoulders and feeling them flex beneath my touch.

"You *are* crazy," he says, pressing a soft kiss on my lips. "Just the right amount."

My heart grows ten sizes.

"Now let's burn this shithole to the ground."

We spend the next twenty minutes dowsing the entire house in gasoline. I smile when he hands me the match. It's a serene scene before us as we watch it go up in flames. Nolan tosses the trash bag containing the Parker's heads into the trunk and then we settle into Michael's car.

"Nolan?"

"Hmm?" he mumbles, his attention fixed on the blazing fire and smokey haze as we drive past.

"What now?"

"I'm not sure."

I nod. "Will you stay with me tonight?"

It takes him a minute to respond. My stomach sinks from the impending rejection, until he takes my hand and brings it to his lips.

"Okay."

Chapter Twenty-Four

Nolan

We wash off and spend the night together at Michael's house. The next morning, Cora has me drop her off at home so she can change and take a nap before work. Another domestic pantomime. I laugh as I drive away from her house in the dead man's car. It was all so easy. So easy to tell Cora a bunch of lines about feeling empty. A bunch of hackneyed psychiatric bullshit that would echo her own pitiful woes.

I'm a monster, Nolan.

No, you're not, Cora. You're just an angry little girl and all it took was one guy with a nice smile to get you to crumble.

It all sounds good as I drive back to Michael's house. Michael's house has very much become a house of corpses, to my delight. I almost want to kill someone in each room of that home, but there won't be enough time.

So do it now. Why are you hesitating? Call the cops and run, now. You'd have so much of a head start. They'd never find you.

I want to see what Cora has planned.

You just want to fuck her again. Admit it. You might even like that little nutcase.

I look in the rearview mirror, my dark eyes gazing back at me. I grin.

"Okay," I tell myself. "Maybe I like her a little."

Cora

It's one of those work shifts where time slows to an agonizing crawl. After a half-hearted nap I stumble into work, blinking sleep from my eyes and wondering why I bothered.

I'm a murderer, now.

I find I like the way that sounds in my head.

As each customer rolls by in an endless conveyor belt of fleshy blobs, mouthing demands at me, waving coupons, suddenly it is all bearable because I have this horrid, wonderful secret.

A murderer just scanned your hand towels for you.

You just asked a killer if the sale lasts all week.

I sink deep into these thoughts, imagining the twisted little faces of each of the customers if I were to stab them like I did Ryan and Michael. I'm still imagining this when a woman steps in front of me and slams a pack of gum down on the counter.

Frizzy hair tied up in a messy ponytail. Red eyes like she's been crying. Her face is contorted in a grimace that tells me that she's holding back a lot of messy anger.

I recognize Natalie immediately, but for fun, I ask if she found everything okay.

She swallows hard as she pays for the gum. It must have taken a huge amount of guts to confront me. My guess is someone saw Nolan and I together. One of her friends saw us talking here, at the store, or in the parking lot, or driving together. Something. It doesn't really matter.

"I was wondering if we could talk?" she asks. "I know it's weird. It's crazy. There are some things I want to know, that's all."

I look her in the eyes, eyebrow cocked. "Nolan and I didn't sleep together while you were dating," I reply. Hopefully that's enough, and she'll scurry off and leave me the fuck alone. In two weeks, she'll be with her high school boyfriend or some vanilla guy who wears basketball shorts and backwards hats, claiming on her social media that "he's everything I've been looking for."

Normal people are terrifying.

"That's not it, that's—that's good to know. No, look, can we talk for a minute? On your lunch break? After work?" Her bottom lip trembles, and briefly I wonder what Nolan could have possibly seen in her.

She's easy to manipulate. Push the right buttons and she'll do whatever you want.

That sinister little voice leaks into my head again. It's sounding more and more like Nolan.

Originally the plan was to lure a female victim for Nolan. The two of us, worshipping him, fulfilling his every fantasy until cutting the little bitch open.

Together.

And wouldn't it be delightful if it was precious Natalie? Seeing her at the party, dragging Nolan around to talk to people, poking him, prodding him, acting like he was a handsome pet.

She has no idea who he is. What he is.

The idea sparkles brilliantly in my mind. I have to seize it.

But I'll have to coax it out of her. Slowly push her into it. I'll have to do what Nolan does; playing with people like the toys they are.

"Fine," I tell Natalie. I nod at the café area. "I'll take my break and meet you over there."

She smiles in relief and murmurs, "Thank you," before walking briskly away, eyes on the floor.

I watch her go as another sinister thought slides into my brain, flaring and blossoming until I can't ignore how aroused it makes me.

I want to play with myself while watching Nolan strangle her.

Chapter Twenty-Five

Cora

She's sitting at the same table Michael and I sat at a few days ago. I sit down across from her and wait for her to speak. Around us, people walk by clutching bags and wheeling carts, an entire sea of normalcy swirling past us as Natalie and I stare across from one another, and I have to wonder if my life can get any more chaotic.

"So, we actually saw each other at the Halloween party. Nolan and I were there. And when he broke up with me, I told my friends, and one of them said she'd seen Nolan here, talking to you."

I can't do this. I don't want to hear the whole recap. I don't want to hear about her feelings.

"Shut up," I spit out. "Just shut the fuck up."

"W-what?"

"Do you want him back or not?"

She blinks twice and rears back, like I slapped her. "I don't understand."

I rub my eyes and try to hold back my mounting frustration. Nolan is right; everything does feel mundane after you've taken a life. Life is so much smaller. And so much more agonizing to withstand.

"You wouldn't have come here," I begin, glaring at her, "if you didn't want him back. You wouldn't be confronting me and sitting down with all your tears and 'poor me' bullshit."

"W-what are you talking about?"

"You don't want to understand what happened. You don't give a fuck. You're just mad that you lost something, and you want it back."

Tears glisten brightly in her eyes, but Natalie doesn't crumple into sobs. I'll give her that. She might look like an honor roll student who wants to save every stray cat, but she's got some guts.

"Fine," she admits. "Yes. I want him back."

I roll my eyes. Nolan's good. He has this one sucked in.

He's got you, too, Cora.

I ignore that and lean in. This part is important. I'm not like Nolan; I don't slink up to people and talk them into whatever I want. I don't have much of a mask to put on to fool people. Cora the loner, Cora the mean girl, Cora who acts like she's better than everyone.

I can't seduce Natalie; even if she is bi-curious, she's firmly fixated on Nolan. But the insecurities... what would Nolan do? He would lean on them. Pull the threads up with his teeth until he had her wet and begging for him.

"You've never been dumped, have you?" I ask.

"What?" Again, startled.

"No boy has ever said no to you. You're attractive, reasonably smart. You go after the nice ones, maybe the ones who are a little shy. They talk to you about, what? Music?"

Natalie leans forward. There's still anger etched on her face but clearly this is the most interesting conversation she's had in years. "Books. Studying."

"And you smile at them and twirl your pretty hair and you have them as much or as little as you want them. Right?"

She shakes her head. Her eyes are wide; like she wants to run... but hearing the truth about herself dripping from my lips has her so intoxicated that she can't.

"It's not like that," she mumbles. "They ask me out, and sometimes I say yes. Sometimes they're nice and we date for a while."

"But you're in control the whole time. You tell them how to dress, how to act, what hobbies you prefer them to have, which friends of theirs you like them to hang out with." I don't know any of this; I'm guessing. I'm connecting loose dots about a caricature of a person I barely know.

She runs a shaky hand through her hair.

"They never stand up to me!" she exclaims. "It's like I'm their *mother* and they're just *boys* who can't take care of themselves, and they have those *eyes* that are so *desperate* for my approval, to let them know they're a good boyfriend. And I start to hate them, after a while. It gets so boring."

She gulps, the tears flowing rapidly now, spilling down her cheeks, a few pooling on the lamented tabletop.

With mild horror, I realize she thinks we're having a bonding moment. Two women sharing war stories about being in the trenches with men. Should I tell her about Michael, listening to my problems, waiting to pounce on me and fuck me the moment I was vulnerable?

"But not with Nolan," she continues. "He's so calm. He knows what he wants. He doesn't need me. He doesn't even *want* me, apparently. And I'm falling apart over it and I don't know what to do. I think, I think that has to be love, right? Falling apart at the thought of losing them?"

I hide my smile. *Oh Natalie, it's going to be so fun watching you die.*

"We're not together," I tell her. "Not exactly. I think I... interest him, and that's it. I'm the exciting, crazy girl, you know. Compared to you." I gesture at her. "You've got it all together. You'll make a fine Martha Stewart clone, whatever. Me. I'm... a little off. And he likes that, for now."

She nods feverishly. "So, do I wait? Do I try to make him jealous by seeing someone else? I don't know what to do."

"You could. Or..." I cock my head to the left, like the idea is just hitting me. "You could show him that you're exciting. A little dangerous. Crazy, even."

Her brows furrow. "What do you mean?"

I can see why Nolan put up with her. It's easy to lead her around, to lay traps and watch her stumble into them. "Sex, Natalie. He's using me for some of the weirdest, kinkiest sex. We fucked in the woods the other day."

Her mouth drops to a thin line and for a moment. Her eyes become slits. She looks feline, almost feral in her barely concealed rage. For that brief flash she's very attractive.

"What I'm saying," I soothe, "is that if you surprise him with something like that, he might see a different side of you and want you back." I pause, then line up the shot that I *know* will reel her in. "If you give him the night of his life, you'll never get rid of him."

That's what everyone wants, right? A homogeneous blob of a relationship. Someone stuck to your fucking skin, melded into you like two colors of Play-Doh smashed together. Someone to inhale your foul breath in the morning and deal with how awful, irritatingly human you are.

"What should I do?" Natalie's tone is flat. Low. She's pissed at me, but now I see something else. The good girl who gets all the best grades is competitive. She wants to win. She wants to take Nolan, rip him right out of my hands.

I almost tell her. I almost tell her about Nolan burying his face between my legs, moaning in pleasure at just the taste of me.

Even better, I almost tell her about him hugging me. Thanking me for unleashing him.

"We've been having threesomes," I say.

"So you're just a whore," she blurts out, waiting for me to react. But I don't. I examine the lines in my palms like I've never seen them before. "That's why he likes you."

I shrug. "At least I'm not boring."

"And I am?"

"He dumped you, didn't he?"

"I hate girls like you," she snarls, wiping away an escaped tear.

"Ditto."

"I know every guy wants to do it with two girls but—"

"Nope," I cut her off. "It was Nolan, another guy, and me."

Her mouth falls open. "Oh."

I resist the urge to blow her a kiss. Natalie just makes you want to be awful to her, doesn't she?

"Nolan's really generous like that. I was thinking of paying him back with a girl. What do you say?"

Uncertainty etches itself across her face. This is going further than she'd ever imagined. The conversation, the one she'd rehearsed, has gotten away from her. But now it's something exciting, and there's a chance to get her precious Nolan back. All she has to do is be a little slutty… like me.

"I guess I could try that," she sniffles. "We would have to sit down and discuss rules and boundaries first—"

"No. None of that bullshit. I'm going to give you an address. You will be there at 9 p.m. You will dress in a black corset. Black boots. You will wear a mask that covers your face. Do you understand?"

She laughs. "Oh-kay, chill out with the dominatrix vibe."

I immediately stand up. I scribble Michael's address on one of the napkins and slide it over to her. I'm enjoying this; this power.

"If you do not show up, I'm going to fuck him so good he will forget you ever existed."

With that, I walk away. I don't even turn back.

I know that she'll be there.

She might even be early.

I'll admit it; I'm anxious.

It's 8:52 p.m. and the house is eerily still, like it's waiting patiently to watch what we are about to do. Nolan seems unbothered; he goes into Michael's office and starts spinning around in the chair, twirling a pen between his fingers.

I'm hoping Natalie does as she's told. There's a pit of unease in my stomach as I wait near the door, checking the window for her every time I think I hear a car.

What if she shows up and isn't wearing a mask? What if she wants to talk to Nolan? If she shows up vulnerable and crying, this will all fall apart.

What if Nolan doesn't want to kill her? What if he takes it as a betrayal and tries to kill me? Fuck it, he might kill us all. He might give up trying to stay ahead of the police and just paint the walls with our blood.

That's not it, is it Cora? You're worried he might actually like her. Just a little. He might like that innocence in her; that innocence you never, ever had.

Headlights flare across the windows.

"Nolan," I say sharply. "Bedroom. Wait for us there."

He ambles out of Michael's office, scratching his head. He's wearing a dark sweater that clings to him tightly and loose jeans that hang low on his hips. His black hair is tangled and messy; he looks etched out of a Calvin Klein ad. "You know that there's a lot of bloodstains in there? I tried cleaning them but uh, it didn't help much."

"Cover them with blankets or something. "

He shrugs and wanders away. In that instance, he seems almost normal. Like any other guy with a slightly demanding girlfriend.

There's a meek knock at the door. I fix my hair and examine myself quickly in the mirror in the hall. I'm wearing a black corset with frilly black panties. Boots that hug the top of my knees. My hair is drawn back, and I've put on a pair of large hoop earrings.

Nolan hasn't complimented me yet. He seems distant. Distracted. And I hate that I notice. And I really hate that I care.

Natalie steps in and as she sets down her bag and takes off her long coat, it is clear she came to play. Her corset is sleek and cinches at her waist tighter than I thought possible. Her makeup is flawless, and her hair is done into pigtails. She's wearing fishnet leggings that crisscross her legs as her thighs strain against them. Her boots go up further than mine, and that bothers me. I hear the heels clunk on the hardwood floor.

"Nice outfit," I tease. "I guess I'm not the only whore, huh?"

She glares at me. "How is this going to work?"

"You brought a mask?"

She nods.

"Put it on." I pull out a long chain with a collar at the end. "Then put this on."

"Oh, come on."

"If it's too much for you, you can leave. I'll wear it for him. He'll love it."

She edges around me, looking deeper into the house, hoping to get a glimpse of him.

"Does he know I'm here?"

I close the gap between us, grabbing either side of her hips and pulling her directly against me. She pulls back slightly, her face drawn in agonizing confusion. I sway my body slowly against hers, the fabric of our outfits rasping against each other.

"Natalie, imagine this. I bring him a masked girl on a leash. A girl who will do anything he says." Natalie's perfume, vanilla and coconut, smells sweet and alluring. The smooth skin of her bare shoulders looks so inviting, I want to press my lips against it. "Then when he's done fucking the living hell out of this obedient slut, he takes the mask off to come on those pretty lips," I kiss her, gently, feeling her freeze in shock, "and realizes it's you."

"Um—"

"Boring old Natalie has a different side he's never seen. A side that matches his. You think he'll let you go after that? Even I see how good you look right now, and I fucking hate you."

She pushes me away but reaches down and fumbles for the mask out of her bag. She pulls it over her head, and I help pull her pigtails through the loops in the latex.

"This is the weirdest thing I've ever done." She tightens the mask and takes the collar from me, moving her necklace out of the way to tighten the collar around her throat. "I feel stupid. Is Nolan even here? I bet this is some joke you're playing."

As if on cue, Nolan, from deep in the house, calls out: "Everything good?"

She gathers her breath to shout an answer, but I cover her mouth. "Yes!" I yell back. "One second!"

She glares at me but falls silent. She's taller than me, the boots making it even more obvious. Still, it's very satisfying to tug on the leash and draw her closer.

"Do what we say, and you'll have him back. I don't want him. This is just a game to me. You can take him back and go play house and join the stupid PTA. I don't care."

We start to head toward Nolan, Natalie walking beside me, but I can't resist rubbing it in. "Oh no. You're going to crawl."

"What?" she hisses.

"Crawl for him, bitch."

To my amazement, she sinks down and begins crawling on her hands and knees, sighing with disdain as she does it.

"I can't believe this."

Me neither, honestly, but it's really starting to turn me on. I can see why Nolan acts like this in the bedroom. It feels incredible. I tug the leash. "You don't have permission to speak. Be a good girl and hurry up."

Nolan is lying on the bed, staring blankly at the ceiling. He's spread a quilt over the mattress, and I see pillows conveniently tossed on the bloodstains that were on the floor.

"I brought something for you." I lead Natalie to the side of the bed. The latex covers her face entirely; only her eyes and mouth are in view. They look pleadingly up at Nolan, but his face is impassive. If he recognizes her, he isn't letting on.

He swings his legs off the bed, so that his thighs are on either side of Natalie as she kneels. Her face is level with his crotch, and I can see his cock stiffening as it presses against the blue-grey denim.

"What's her name?" he asks softly. He begins slowly pushing up his sleeves, revealing his forearms.

"She doesn't deserve a name. She's only here for one purpose."

"Hm." He reaches down and grips her by the chin. "You want me to use you, huh?"

She nods, but blissfully remains quiet. All the resistance and attitude went out the window the moment she saw him. She hungrily eyes Nolan. She's bought into the fantasy.

He takes the metal chain and stands up. He wraps it once, twice around his closed fist, and uses it to force her to stand up as well. He glances at me, and his eyes are blank. Unreadable.

He knows. He knows and he's playing along.

For now.

The insecurity spikes again, and I fight to stay calm. I can feel it roaring in my brain, shrieking at me that he's going to choose her. Look at her! How could he ever choose me? She's softer and prettier. She's everything he could want. I really *was* the crazy distraction and the moment he starts fucking her, I will be gone. Wiped from his mind. I'll cease to exist.

Nolan moves suddenly, with violent ferocity. For a second, I think he's just going to kill her immediately, that he's done holding back and he's ready to descend into whatever void that hides behind his eyes.

He shoves her onto the bed and rips the panties off. I hear one of the seams in the waistband split. He holds her down with one hand while the other tears off his belt, his pants falling to his knees as he slides into her and begins fucking her savagely. There's nothing patient or gentle about it.

"Oh *yes*!" Natalie exclaims. She's face down on the bed, her entire body rocking back and forth with the force of Nolan. He's breathing in short, angry pants as he tears his shirt off before grabbing both of her hips and bending his knees slightly so he can get deeper inside of her.

None of this is how it was supposed to go. I wasn't supposed to feel this awful twinge of jealousy deep in my gut. I wasn't supposed to be standing here awkwardly during this threesome. My sense of control has been snatched away and I don't know what to do.

"Please, *harder*!" Natalie begs.

"Shut the fuck up so I can come," he says coldly. Then he groans angrily, closing his eyes and running his fingertips down her back.

I haven't moved.

He snaps his head in my direction. "You." He pulls out of her and looks at me. "Clean me. With your mouth. Now."

I don't like being talked to like this, but at the same time, I have his attention while Natalie tries to catch her breath on the bed. Maybe I can get control of this situation again. Maybe I can win over Nolan right now. The panicked insecurity has come over me entirely; I *have* to win.

Dropping to my knees, I stare up at him through my lashes. The second I wrap my fingers around his cock and make a move to suck him into my mouth, he reaches down and cups my face with his hands.

My heart pounds like a drum in my chest. He caresses my cheekbones with his thumbs and studies my face, stepping closer. It feels like my body is now on fire, and I might spontaneously combust at any given moment. The blood rushes to the tips of my fingers as I tighten my grip on his straining erection.

He hasn't come yet.

He's been saving it just for me.

My mouth becomes dry, and I swallow nervously, staring up at him with a feeling I've never felt before. Admiration. Loyalty.

"Cora," he breathes.

My knees begin to wobble and every breath I take sounds a thousand times louder than the one before. Suddenly the bed squeaks, and Natalie drops to her knees beside me. Nolan turns his head and locks his eyes with hers.

"Fucking bitch," I snarl, "this was our moment and you ruined it!"

Nolan pats Natalie on the head.

"Now, now. Wait your turn." He turns back to me and thrusts into my hand. "Show her how it's done, Cora." With that, he spits on his dick.

My lips slide all the way down his length, and I take him deep into the back of my throat, gagging loudly. He fists my hair, and a growl erupting from his chest as he pumps into my mouth. I cradle my tongue against his cock and suck him harder, taking him deeper, until I'm choking on him. Tears leak from my eyes as he fucks my throat, and I bob my head faster, meeting his urgent thrusts.

The saliva thickens in my mouth and drool coats my chin. Suddenly he's burying my fingers in my hair and yanking me onto the bed. He lays on his back and shoves himself up into my mouth once more.

He motions with a wave of his hand for Natalie to join us. I eye her closely as she crawls onto the mattress. I work him harder and faster with my mouth and hand, until he pulls the bitch onto him, her thighs now straddling his head. She sits on his face and begins to ride his tongue, and without warning, her eyes lock with mine.

I hold him in the very back of my throat, gagging silently, widening my eyes as hers turn to small slits. She's taunting me.

She's fucking taunting me.

Ha-ha! I get to ride his face!

He groans into her pussy and grips her thighs, holding her in place as he devours her. She cries and whimpers in utter satisfaction, rocking her hips back and forth, grinding against him. He exhales sharply, digging his nails into her skin.

My gaze lowers from her, to him, and I watch in envy as he works magic on her pussy with his tongue, sucking and nibbling on her clit. There's a dull ache that settles between my legs and I begin to imagine it's me.

It's me he's tongue fucking.

It's me he's getting off.

She cries out in awe, right on cue, planting her palms firmly on his chest to keep herself upright. God, she comes so hard. Her body convulses. She gasps, grinding against his wet lips as he nuzzles his nose and mouth in her needy cunt.

The moment he strains his neck and leans up to press a tender kiss on her pink, swollen clit, a rush of pure anger and adrenaline rises inside me.

Natalie glares at me with hatred. "Mine," she murmurs, clawing at his masculine, bare chest with her long, pink polished nails. "Nolan. Is. Mine."

I nearly grit my teeth out of anger. Nolan feels it, and growls, shoving Natalie off him and sitting up and regarding me with an open hostility that is both terrifying and devastatingly attractive. It's a look that tells me he'd do anything to me, and not think twice about it.

"What's your problem?" he demands, grabbing hold of me. "Are you not getting enough attention?"

"I—"

Yes, Nolan. That's exactly it. I want your attention. I want you so deep inside me you forget other women exist. I want to feel your cock flex when you orgasm, and I want to know that it was me that made that happen and that it is me, only ME who makes you feel that good. I want to be in every dirty, sick thought you have. I want to seep into your fucking soul. Fuck my ass, fuck my face, do whatever you want to me as long as you're doing it to me and only me.

I can't say that. I can't even finish a sentence. I can't tip my hand and let him know how much power he has over me. If he knows, he might lose interest. I'll stop being the fascinating monster he has taken a shine to.

I'll be another Natalie.

He leaps up, forcing me backwards away from the bed, our bodies touching, eyes locked together the entire time. Then he slips behind me, his arms encircling my waist and his chin resting on my shoulder.

"Oh, is she jealous?" Natalie's voice is grating as she sits up proudly on her knees, watching us. "Nolan, come here."

"Lie on your back. And take that stupid mask and chain off, Natalie. I knew it was you the moment you walked in here."

She glares at me but does as he says, tugging the mask off and rotating herself to lay back and watch us, her legs dangling over the side of the bed.

"Now what I'm going to do with you?" Nolan breathes beside my ear. "This was your idea. You set this up. Now that it's happening... what? You're jealous? Is she right?"

His arms are warm and tight around me as he slowly pushes me back toward the bed.

"Yes," I whisper. "It made me jealous, seeing you with her."

"That's really hot," he mutters. He shoves me onto Natalie, urging me to climb on her, my hair hanging over her like a shroud. He makes me straddle her waist and presses his hand against the small of my back, so I lay against her.

My face looms over hers, and I can feel the hatred baking off her. Our hair tangles together, a fusion of harsh black against her light brown. She's biting down on her lip; a tiny white edge of the tooth digging into her lipstick so hard I can see it crack.

"Nolan?" Natalie looks around me to look at him. "What are you doing?"

His voice is mild; amused. "I'm going to fuck Cora's brains out right on top of you. If you're good, you can lick my cum out of her."

The look of shock, outrage, and humiliation that cuts across her face makes it hard to breathe. I can see why Nolan is the way he is. The power in being able to hurt people.

His words have me drenched, and when he slides into me, I'm on the verge of orgasm. After several rough thrusts I'm crying out, burying my face in Natalie's neck as she turns away. Her humiliation and frustration makes it better for me, and I can't help but giggle between moans of pleasure.

Nolan pulls me back up, holding both of my arms, his balls slapping the back of my thighs while he thrusts harder and harder.

Then he starts complimenting me.

"Do you know how *fucking* sexy you are? I love every curve of this body. Every mark and moment of it. This freckle on your shoulder—" He kisses it and I groan, arching my back. "—this spot just below your neck—" He kisses that, too. "—this ass."

He slaps it—hard—and the shock of it makes me smile.

"When you look at me when you're pissed off, with that little scar on your lip, all of it turns me on so *fucking* much."

Natalie's face is twisting in disgust at what we're doing on top of her. The spell is broken for her, and it is delicious to watch the panic wash over her.

"Am I your whore, Nolan? Tell me I'm your whore." I look down at Natalie. Some of my drool is on her neck.

"You're my whore, Cora. You're my filthy little whore."

Something about having him obey me sends me flying over the edge. I clench hard around him, slamming back onto him as hard as I can.

Natalie starts to move, shaking her head as she breaks away from us, clawing her way to the edge of the bed.

Nolan is still fucking me, pulling his dick nearly all the way out of me just to ram it back in.

"The knife," I gasp at him, "in my left boot."

He shoves himself all the way into me and holds himself there as his hand fumbles to my leg, pulling the knife out by the hilt and pressing it into my hand.

Her eyes bulge out of her head with horror as I quickly reach her way, slitting her throat from ear to ear, blood pouring out steadily from the gaping slit.

"Now," I say between clenched teeth, "he will never be yours."

Nolan spins me around as his thrusts become frantic, the entire bed shaking as Natalie gurgles, her throat now a real-life waterfall of red. She collapses onto the mattress beside us, her head next to mine, clutching at her neck and trying to scoop the blood back inside the open wound, although it continues to trickle through her fingers.

Switching our positions, I straddle Nolan's hips, positioning the head of his cock at my entrance and stare into his eyes deeply.

"Tell me, Nolan," I plead, lowering myself onto him slowly, inch by inch, until I'm entirely consumed with him.

He grips my waist, and his mouth falls open.

"Yours," he confirms, growing harder inside me. "Fuck... Cora... I'm yours, and you're mine."

"Yes," I encourage, rolling my hips, and building up speed as I ride him. "Nolan—I—"

He reaches up and presses his palm over my lips, silencing me. I lock my eyes with Nolan's and begin bouncing on his thick cock. The bed squeaks. The headboard slams against the wall. Natalie groans with terror.

Nolan and I come together, crying out euphorically. He sits up and wraps his arms around my frame, holding me close as I slow my pace, rolling my hips in small, precise circles.

I run my bloody hands through his hair, and he presses his forehead against mine, breathing me in. My orgasm swallows me whole. Here we are, embracing one another and coming hard while his annoying bitch of an ex bleeds out on the bed beside us.

How utterly romantic!

My heart fucking pounds.

With his fingertips, he traces gentle patterns on my lower back before framing my face with his hands. His eyes meet mine. There are grins on our faces as we both wait for the other to look away. My stomach sinks when I realize neither of us are going to.

"Kiss me," I gasp.

Abruptly, Natalie rolls onto the floor, making a mess, and our lips collide.

Chapter Twenty-Six

Cora

"I can hear your brain chewing on itself." He turns over on his side and props his head up on his fist, gazing at me. "What are you thinking about?" Nolan asks, breaking me from my thoughts.

I'm thinking about how much my life has changed since I met him. He's shown me that it's okay to be myself. That there is nothing wrong with me. That I am fine just the way I am.

For all these years, I've always felt different from everyone else. But when I look at Nolan, it's like looking into a mirror. I have this image of us as black shadows, lurking in dark alleys and weaving between crowds of people. Like vampires.

Monsters.

I play around with these thoughts in my mind, when suddenly, he takes my jaw in his hand and turns me to face him. I stare into his eyes.

"You're being quiet," he observes, tracing my lips with his thumb.

"Am I?"

He nods.

My brain doesn't know how to pivot and throw something back at him. My whole life, I've been so entirely against making any real connections with people. I tried to care about Jerald, but all of that went out the window the second I realized it was never about him to begin with.

I wasn't mad that my friend was murdered.

I was mad that I never had the balls to do it myself.

It would have been so easy.

Aside from Jerri, Nolan is the closest I've ever been to connecting with someone. He understands me on this deep, sensual level. He *sees* me. He sees the darkness inside me and embraces it with open arms.

The same, twisted urge I feel to strangle customers; that itching of violence that writhes inside of me, has been tamed into attraction. Aimed at Nolan.

And I'm so hungry for him.

It terrifies me.

"Cora," he breathes, brushing my bangs out of my eyes. "Talk to me."

"I don't know what to say."

"Just say what's on your mind."

I rest my face on his bare chest and take in his warmth. "I... I think I care about you." My words are doing that thing where they fail to capture what I mean.

His body tenses and his hand in my hair becomes still.

"I think I might want you," I admit. "For... a while." I did it again, pulling back and changing words at the last second, giving out a flattened, Diet Coke flavor of what I wanted to say.

"A while," he echoes.

I rest my chin on his shoulder while searching his eyes. He appears calm… much calmer than I anticipated. He's not throwing me off him. He's not running in the other direction.

He's not stabbing me.

That must be a good sign.

"Well?" I ask.

"Well, what?"

"Aren't you going to say something?"

His jaw tightens. "I'm not good at finding the words."

"Neither am I," I agree. "But… I'm trying… because I want you, Nolan, and when I want something… I go for it. So, here I am, going for it."

"You want me to tell you how I care about you," he lets out. "How you're the first thing I see when I open my eyes in the morning, and the last thing I see before I go to bed. How I think about you every second of every day and can't get you out of my head no matter how hard I try."

"I want the truth."

He frames my face with his hands and kisses me softly. I breathe him in, my heart thumping hard in my chest.

"The truth," he whispers against my lips, "is that you're a threat. You're burning down everything I had planned." He slides upward and draws me against his chest, crushing me against him with both of his arms. His lips mumble against my forehead as he continues. "And yet, I'm still here. I'm still playing this game with you, and I don't want to stop."

His hands find my throat and I'm pulled back to eye level. Our legs intertwine, our thighs parting and embracing each other. Nolan closes his eyes and gently leans his forehead against mine. "You scare me."

I stare at his closed eyelids as he kisses me again, passionately, dipping his tongue inside my mouth, tasting me eagerly.

"Nolan," I moan, digging my fingertips into the back of his neck. "You scare me, too."

"Run away with me."

"Okay. When?"

"Baby steps, little monster." He stands, lifting me into his arms. "For now, let's wash off."

He steps over Natalie's lifeless body and the pool of blood on the floor. I find myself touching him as he walks us to the bathroom—a romantic gesture, and now a part of our routine after kills. He places me onto my feet in the shower and turns on the water.

There's a pungent smell of blood that rises along with the steam, sweet and metallic. The water runs red as we stand beneath the stream of hot water. It feels amazing against my skin, soothing my sore arm and back muscles. I'm out of shape. Stabbing takes a lot of strength, that's for sure.

I watch Nolan closely as he tilts back his head and shuts his eyes, beads of water dripping down his face steadily and soaking his hair. He runs his hands through the strands, his biceps flexing, and a muscle in his jaw twitches. He appears so deep in his thoughts. It's like I'm not even here.

I step forward, pressing myself against him, tracing my fingers along the contours of his firm body. My fingers linger over the barely healed cut on his shoulder. It feels so rough against my delicate touch. The image of me burying the knife into his flesh comes to mind.

"I hurt you," I nearly whisper, my chest tightening.

He lowers his head and immediately locks his eyes with mine. Squinting through droplets of water, he presses his lips into a firm, straight line.

"I'm... I'm sorry." I wonder if he knows how bizarre it feels to apologize. Understanding you've done damage to someone and caring enough to want to atone for it.

He blinks at me, disoriented. "What?"

"For stabbing you the other night." I cup his face with my hand. "I'm sorry."

"Don't be." Leaning into my palm, he squeezes his eyes shut, his body stiffening against me. "I'm not."

Without warning, he grabs my throat and moves me backwards, pinning my back to the cold wall of the shower. Grazing my fingertips along the curve of his hips, I pull him against me, closing the space between us. A heated tension builds and builds, until we can't take it anymore. Our lips collide, tongues lashing, teeth clattering.

His fingers tighten around my throat to the point where I can no longer breathe. I kiss him back, clawing at his hand. Suddenly he spins me around and bends me over, spreading my legs with his knee. I press my palms against the wall, and he slams into me aggressively.

"I'm not sorry, Cora," he grunts between thrusts. "I'm. Not. Fucking. Sorry."

Nolan

Natalie's body is in Michael's trunk as I drive it to the trainyard.

I always read about other serial killers. Depraved lunatics doing all sorts of delightful things. Gutting hikers and leaving their bodies in the woods. Genius! No carrying, no hauling! Just snatch the life out of them and cartwheel away.

But no, Nolan has to be elaborate. He has to play with the bodies and cut off parts of them. He has to bring Cora on fucking field trips and let her pick victims and fuck everything up.

There was a woman in the '90s who killed her husband and cooked his head in the oven. Put his remains in the garbage disposal. The neighbors said her disposal ran for hours; they could hear it.

That's what I need, a giant garbage disposal.

I close my eyes and imagine the shredded, raw hamburger meat texture of Michael, Natalie, Ryan, and Jerald, their bones crunching like rock salt under your boot in wintertime, the blood and viscera turning into a milkshake paste. I would lay under it and let the storm of blood cover me, coating me so thickly I could hardly breathe.

It's nice to be alone, though.

There's a small Ziploc bag with a few stray hairs—Cora's—in my pocket. I'll place them around the room I killed Jerald and Michael in. I'll wipe down the tools and everything I've touched. That, plus the skin under the fingernails of each body...

It's loose. I'll need to do more.

I need... a witness.

Not a witness so much as someone the police can interview to help shade the case my way; I'm a victim. I've been killed and they can't find my body.

Holding the steering wheel with one hand I pull out my phone. There's a litany of missed messages; parents, Natalie asking about Cora, a girl from a different class asking about notes.

And Jay.

Asking if I want to get drinks and watch basketball.

Perfect.

I text him back and make plans. I'll tell him about Cora. Cora being crazy. Cora stalking me. Cora having a knife collection.

Jay will dismiss it. But when I disappear, and the police track down my acquaintance...

"Nolan? Yeah, I saw him. We just hung out the other day. He said he was seeing this Cora girl, but she was a little intense for him. Clinger vibes, you know. Said she had knives? He seemed kinda worried about it. Is he okay?"

That's all I would need to angle a detective toward Cora.

And a quick, anonymous tip that I'd heard screaming coming from the trainyard... with the way the bodies were rotting, the smell alone would lead them right to the container.

"It's loose," I mutter to the car. "It's loose but it'll work."

"What's loose?" someone croaks, and I jump, the steering wheel jerking sideways, making me fight to keep the car straight, while whirring my head around to see who spoke.

There's no one in the car.

I keep my eye on the rearview mirror. Waiting.

Because a solitary auditory hallucination is one thing. An aberration in my reality. You can write it off. Ignore it. A sound wave bounced off the leather seats, echoed in an unusual way, fused with the ambient sounds of a car engine... and managed to produce a voice.

Fine. The great propaganda machine of telling myself I was alright could get to work.

So, what was that scratching sound?

In the back seat, like rats, the sound my own nails made when I ran them down my face, catching on the stubble after a few days of not shaving.

I clear my throat, eyeing the backseat.

There's a long pause; long enough that I start to be relieved. It's been a few days without a lot of sleep, and a lot of stress. Maybe I'm simply frayed at the ends and imagining things.

Scritch-scratch.

Scritch-scratch.

The scratching occurs with horrifying frequency as the fabric of the backseat bulges and pulses as something presses on it from the other side. A rat? A squirrel? I would've seen one when dumping Natalie in there.

A low *brrrrr* as a gash opens in the fabric. I see a finger slip out, wriggling like a worm in the dirt. Then a second finger emerges. Followed by the rest of an entire human hand.

I recognize the nail polish. That shouldn't matter, because there's only one body in the trunk, but somehow seeing the pink nail polish reflecting streetlights as we drive under them made it tangible.

I rub my eyes.

The hand is gone.

I laugh, shakily, then fully twist in my seat, looking for the hole.

A singular blue eye gazes at me.

In a tone that sounds like I'm telling a child that they need to go back to bed, I say, "Natalie, sweetie, we killed you. You're dead."

There's a great, hideous rummaging as she apparently turns herself over in the trunk, thudding her feet on the lid. I glance at the road, and then back at the horror show in the back seat.

Her tongue is sticking out of the fabric now.

"Look, Nolan," she rasps, "I made a gloryhole, just for you. Do you like me now?"

"You were never that funny when you were alive, Natalie." My tone is quiet and controlled. I'm proud of myself for that. My hands are gripping the steering wheel very tightly.

"Oh," she pouts. "Why do you gotta be so mean?" She gags wetly, and I hear a glob of something smack as it splatters against the seat.

I shouldn't look, but I do.

It isn't blood, exactly. A thick, greenish-yellow liquid gleams in a puddle, quivering with each bump the car hits.

It smells faintly acidic.

Like orange juice.

"That's bile. Bile and probably a little bit of your cum. I felt it when I was blowing you." She sighs. "I thought if I made you come before she did, you'd pick me over her. Instead, you two did something very, very nasty to me."

There's a straight patch of road ahead and no cars around. I take a deep breath, hold it in and shut my eyes.

One.

Two.

Three.

I breathe out.

I check the road.

I breathe again.

Then I look in the backseat.

Natalie's entire head is sticking through. Upside down and smeared with more bile as she hangs upside down, jostling with the motion of the car. Her hair hangs to the floor, clumped with black clots of blood. They remind me of black flies, snarled in a spider's web.

"I'm not going anywhere, No-lan."

I nod. Okay. I hallucinate now. Mental illness symptoms tend to manifest in the mid-to-late twenties. Okay. This is mine. I have...

Ex-girlfriend corpse hallucinations.

I focus on the road, tracing the yellow median line with my eyes, holding it steady, willing Natalie away. There's a worrying knot working in my stomach. How soon until I start seeing Jerald, and

Michael, and Ryan? Will I be seeing everyone I kill? Digging themselves out of the ground and out of the walls just to taunt me?

Eyes on the road.

Eyes on the backseat. She's gone.

Eyes back to the road.

Eyes to the backseat.

She's pulled herself midway out, but her hips are stuck and she's using her bloody hands to widen the gap so she can squeeze through. Her bare breasts flop and dangle as she strains to free herself. She catches my eye and grins widely, liquid spewing between her teeth.

My eyes go back to the road. I refuse to turn my head despite all the choked gasping and groans I hear as she tries to get out of the trunk.

She can't hurt me. She's dead. She's been dead for hours. If she was going to get up and move around, she would've when Cora and I were laying together in bed. This isn't. You got a sick mind, baby, that's it. A sick mind. Most of the time it just makes you want to bite people, but right now it's biting you. And you know what? That's fine. We can roll with that. Your mind wants to play games? Okay. Let's play.

Out of the side of my vision I watch her pull herself into the front seat. For a brief moment, the gash in her throat flaps at me like a hungry mouth, the edges of the wound clapping together. Old blood oozes out like thick chocolate syrup.

It reeks.

It reeks of shit and rot and that fridge I cleaned out with my dad.

Then she's sitting next to me, like I'm taking her to dinner. She crosses her bare legs and examines her nails, waiting for me to speak.

There's blood down her neck and chest, a large crimson streak that extends down her hip, and along her thigh, ending in a skinny drizzle that encircles her ankle.

I've seen Natalie alive, in lingerie, asking me to join her on the bed. I've had her on her knees, adoring me with those big eyes.

She's never looked more attractive than right now.

"What do you want, Natalie?"

"Nothing much, babe. Just wondering how this all ends."

"What are you talking about?"

She taps her fingertips on the hand rest. "Can you really leave her?"

"Yes."

"Ooh, you say it so easily. Yet every step of the way she's dragged you in closer." Her voice drops in pitch. It's my voice, my words, drifting out of her dead mouth. "*Cora, you're the only thing that scares me.*"

I glance at her. One of her eyes is stuck; one is aimed at me, the other drooping and gazing at the floor. She looks like a broken doll. "Lying to Cora is as easy as lying to you. Fucking her is just a bit better, that's all. She has a better ass."

Her bloody, seasick grin widens. "Fucking her is one thing. Murdering your ex-girlfriend together? That looks like loyalty to me."

"Whatever it looks like, it'll be over soon."

"Maybe." Natalie's voice changes. It's Cora's now. Huskier, less nasally. Better. "Or maybe you'll have a change of heart at the last moment."

"Yeah, that's me. I'm real big on change of heart."

I hit a deep pothole on purpose. Natalie slips sideways and bounces her head on the passenger window. She giggles. "Nolan and Cora sitting in a tree. K-I-S-S-I-N-G."

Her voice is digging into my brain. I can feel reality tremble. I want to dive into the rolling blackness and let it feast, but I can't.

I need to break the hallucination; I need to get control.

"Natalie, I think you look better now that you're dead."

The hallucination freezes. Like a video trying to buffer. "Oh, yeah?"

"Yeah, baby. Why don't you open up that mouth and put my dick in it?"

"I know what you're doing," she mumbles.

"How about I fuck that open slit in your throat? Hmmm? Or I could plunge my knife into your stomach right now. It's never too late. Let me get in those guts, baby."

The hallucination bursts out laughing. I assume it's because I am laughing.

I wipe tears from my eyes and laugh harder, and when I look over again Natalie is gone.

When I stick her fucking ugly body in a barrel, she's quiet. She's quiet when I wipe down my knives and kill tools. She's quiet when I plant Cora's hair around the shipping container.

I enjoy the cold silence.

Chapter Twenty-Seven
Nolan

Somehow, this is the most difficult part. Jay sits next to me at the bar, our faces awash in the glow of a half-dozen flat screens as basketball players in bright jerseys run up and down the court.

To my horror, I realize I've gotten used to Cora. For the last few days, outside of our victims, she's been the one I've been talking to the most. I've grown to appreciate the way we can talk openly about the blood and the rage.

I'm having trouble putting on the human mask.

"Where you been, man? What's been going on?" Jay asks. "I honestly can't believe we're hanging out. I didn't think you liked me that much."

"I'm just busy a lot. I've been seeing this girl. She's a handful. Honestly, I needed a break."

"Oh, yeah? That Natalie girl?"

I'm very pleased that he remembers Natalie. I wonder if I'm the closest thing he has to a friend.

He'll be such a good witness.

"No, we split, actually. Haven't seen her in a while. I started hooking up with this Cora girl." I smile. "Cute but, woah. Crazy, you know? Like immediately fell in love with me."

Jay nods emphatically. He knows exactly what I mean. Every guy has a crazy girl story. Their mom is crazy, their ex is a psycho. That teacher in high school was a lunatic; that woman that didn't want to date them is batshit. It's a universal, recognized truth amongst men, and when I affirm this belief for Jay, validating his worldview, he'll eagerly spill it out to any male cop that comes around asking questions.

"I once had a girl steal my wallet," Jay says. "Maxed out all my cards. I had to call this company and get the charges removed. It was a pain in the ass."

I order another round of beers. "Get this... we're in bed one night and she starts telling me she has fantasies about *killing* people. And not in that fun way, like how you joke about killing your coworkers and stuff. I think she means it."

"That's a crazy girl for sure." He fixes his backwards cap and grins at me. "But is she hot though?"

"Wouldn't be talking about her if she wasn't."

It goes on like this for a while. I find myself looking around the bar, and for one exhilarating moment I think I see Cora lurking in the shadows, but when I look again, she's gone.

I see Natalie too, briefly, walking in with a crowd of loud college girls, but she disappears just as Cora does.

Jay asks what kind of video games I play, and I can't help but think about the kind of games I want to play with his corpse.

Finally, he starts making the standard noise of "got a lot to do, tomorrow's a long day" and I nod, making the standard responses. We pay and start heading toward the door.

I walk him to his car and then double back, a wide grin breaking off my face.

This bar still has a pay phone. The plastic receiver is chipped and covered in graffiti, but it has a dial tone.

It takes me a minute, but I figure out how to work it. The quarters go in, and using my cell phone, I pull up the police department's anonymous tip line.

The line clicks, and a smooth female voice instructs me to leave a detailed message at the tone. It assures me that this is anonymous, safe, and completely confidential. I am not being recorded in any way.

Still, I raise my voice into a mock falsetto and drop some of my consonants. "Hey, I wanna let someone know there's a lotta noise out by the river, at that old trainyard? I walk my dog by there sometimes and I think I heard yellin'. Could be kids up to somethin'. I dunno. Thanks."

I hang up the phone. Excitement is flooding my body now.

All I have to do is go home, grab my stuff, the little stash of money I have saved, and I am gone. I can take a new name, a new life, a new city full of potential victims.

What about Cora?

It doesn't matter. It's easier now that I'm in motion. Now that I'm away from her. It would be impossible to turn down those eyes, that warmth, the very scent of her. I can admit that.

But freedom. True freedom. Solitude. It's all a few short hours away.

There's yellow caution tape on my door.

I approach it warily, checking around my shoulder for SWAT teams and stern-faced police officers, but I already know it isn't them. They need warrants, paperwork, and an entire system to come together to take any sort of action. I would've been tracked down and questioned long before this step.

I push the crisscrossing layers of tape aside and enter my apartment. I try to do it quietly, but of course the keys jingle, the door clicks, and the floorboards creak.

She's draped the tape all over the place. It lays over my couch and coffee table like a dead snake. It hangs from the ceiling fan and loops around the kitchen chairs.

I see a shoe, then socks, and then a blouse in a loose winding path leading to my bedroom door. It's propped open slightly and a soft red light emanates from it. Music plays gently.

I bite back a laugh. Cora has Halloween store taste.

I begin undressing as I move toward my room, dropping clothes behind me as I follow Cora's trail. I nudge open the door. My mind oscillates between an alarm siren thought of *this is a bad idea* and this other feral desire to see what she's going to do, to see what I'm going to do. The game is escalation and I want to see how far we both can go.

That part wins when I see her on the bed. She's taken everything off and wrapped herself in more caution tape. It weaves over her curves and between her breasts in a loose harness. She's tied a collar out of it around her throat.

She smirks when I enter, spreading her legs and letting me see underneath the crude skirt she's crafted out of the tape. She's twirling a knife and beckoning for me to come closer.

"People say to watch out for red flags in dating, but I figure maybe we should be wrapped in—"

"Caution tape," I finish. "Very clever, Cora."

I'm already giving in... I can feel it. It's easy to dismiss her when she's not around. When I'm not holding her in my arms and feeling her against my skin. When she's a problem, an obstacle to be stepped over—

But then she bites my earlobe and forces me down onto the bed and I'm not fighting it. It is nice, letting her take control. To disengage the whirring, maniacal brain and watch Cora work, let her be devoted and worshipful. She makes me feel like a god.

She loops a strand of the tape around each of my wrists and urges me to raise my hands above my head, tying them to the headboard. They're a bit too tight, and they're cutting off my circulation. It'll take me a minute to get out of them.

It's pretty basic. Plain, really, but she's eager. The last few days have shown that I can teach her.

I'm telling myself this as she leans back and moans, guiding my cock into her. And yeah, the way she works her hips and smiles when I groan makes my resolve to leave without her seem foolish.

Why end this? I want to fuck her in every corner of the globe, leaving a trail of corpses behind us at each one.

"Do you like this?" she pants.

"Yes, baby. I fucking love it. Keep going."

"Say please. I like it when you beg."

"Please, Cora. Don't stop."

"You like it when I'm your good girl?"

"Yes. Yes." I close my eyes and lean my head back and let her do the work. Give this up? What was I thinking?

She's still holding the knife as she grabs my face with both of her hands, her teeth gritted together as I begin thrusting my hips upward to meet her.

"Oh, Cora, when I get out of this, the things I'm going to do to you..."

"Yeah? Like frame me?"

Her words come out in a moan, but the expression on her face is that of wicked triumph. The knife is flush against my face, and the bolt of exhilaration I feel is the same as when you run a red light and narrowly miss getting decimated at an intersection.

It's a lightning strike of mortality.

I lunge against the caution tape and hear it strain, but it holds me just long enough for her to flip the knife around and slam it into my side. The blade scrapes against my ribs as it wedges between them, and suddenly I have no air.

A whistling sound drifts out when I try to scream in pain, but it's like I've been punched in the chest and I. Just. Can't. Get. My. Breath. Back.

One hand works free, and I shove her off me. It goes to the knife, buried in about halfway. I grip the handle, groan, and lean back again, bouncing my head off the wall.

Get it out, get it out, get it out, get it out, it HURTS!

I want to. I want to appease that shrieking voice, but I need to leave it in. It might be the only thing keeping my lung from deflating completely.

"I heard you," Cora says, tears streaming down her face. "I heard you report the bodies. I heard you with Jay. You were going to leave me."

She doesn't care about being framed. She's mad that I was going to leave her. Huh.

Blood is leaking hotly down my side. It feels like someone spilled coffee all over me.

She's stomping around the house, pulling on clothes. She waves the wad of cash in front of me while I try to crawl off the bed, but every move sends horrifying, blossoming black dots before my eyes. I can't pass out. If I pass out, I die.

"Cora, baby, I—"

"I thought we were going to do this together. Be together." There's a stillness in her voice the signals a dichotomy in her. Even as tears well up and pour out of her eyes, even as she clenches her fists around the money, her voice remains steady. As if she expected this.

"C-Cora—"

She wipes away the wetness from her cheeks and stares down at the mixture of blood and tears on her fingers, taken aback.

She turns to leave but stops by the doorframe. I notice she doesn't have my keys; she has Michael's.

"Mutual monsters, right?" She jingles the keys and waves the money I was going to take. "Frame me. That's fine. Tell them all the nasty things I did. And when you're reading headlines about the nasty things I keep on doing, think about me."

I can only stare at her while I'm sliding off the bed in a wet *thud*.

Then, wonder of all wonders, she crosses the room abruptly. Her hand digs at my side, and I scream in her face, my hands frantically trying to beat her away.

She steps back smoothly and takes her handfuls of blood and begins painting the wall over my bed. In jagged letters, she scrawls:

I LOVE YOU

Then, amazingly, she blows me a kiss and saunters out of the room.

Did I just get dumped?

Cora

My hand is on the doorknob when I notice a pink box with a bow on it, sitting on Nolan's kitchen table. I glance quickly down the hall, expecting to see Nolan, bloody and naked, sprinting at me with an axe, except there's only darkness.

There's a note on the lid. It reads "Cora" and then there's a brief, hasty line like he gave up on writing something.

Inside, there's a mask made from flesh.

I recognize Jerald's skin tone immediately. And of course, I recognize Michael's, having had that face pressed against mine. There's even some stubble left on one of the jigsaw patches of cheek flesh.

Nolan groans in the bedroom. I hear a thud. He's more alive than I expected.

Two choices spring to life before me as I slip on the mask made of men.

I could walk into that bedroom and execute the man I love. On some level, I think he'd respect me more. I'd be the monster he always wanted to be.

Jingling the car keys, I twirl in a delirious circle, the mask warm on my face, the eye holes muffling my vision. Narrowing it. There's a chemical smell fusing with the acrid scent of dead flesh, and it mats my hair to my head.

I take it off—putting it back in its box—and look down at its mutated features. There are holes in it. Spots where new skin will need to be added.

My second choice glows in neon.

Run. Take the car. The mask. The violence. Disappear into what Nolan called the American abyss.

And kill as many as I can.

I take the steps two at a time, stuffing the pink box into my bag full of Nolan's money. Michael's car keys jingle cheerfully as I slide into the front seat and music clicks on.

It's time to go.

No more Jerald. No more Michael.

No more *Nolan*.

I adjust the mirror as I back out of the driveway and the song on the radio yells at me about how breakups are tough.

He thought he had everything planned out, shaping me into the perfect little killer, all while planning to dump all the murders on me so he could run off into the sunset. I pull out the box and set it onto the passenger seat. The horizon greets me, and I wonder what the newspapers will call me. I wonder if Nolan will be jealous.

"Breakups are tough," I mumble as the car accelerates away from my hometown.

I will be a new monster soon.

Little did he know, little naïve Cora was always one step ahead.

Nolan

I hear the door slam and a car start up. The tires squeal as she speeds away. My phone is on the table in the living room. I start a wheezing, agonizing crawl toward it, favoring my left side, pulling myself along, gripping the tiny fibers of my carpet for leverage. Tears of pain stream down my face, but through it all, I'm laughing.

I didn't see it coming! A total surprise! Never thought she'd do it! Incredible!

In the hallway, I almost give up. I know I'm not drawing anywhere near enough oxygen, and the amount of blood I'm losing seems to be too much. The world swims around me. I see Natalie again, sitting in my living room, watching me with interest.

I cough, shocking ripples of pain shooting up my side, and she becomes Cora.

When I look again, it's Jerald.

I've gotta calm down. I close my eyes briefly and reach out to that detached part of myself. That part that can rip the fingernails off of people with casual interest. The part that was always assured of its place atop humanity.

Coolly, it tells me that yes, I am in danger.

Although I'm still breathing, somewhat. I can hear a frightening rattle each time I pull air, a sickly sound that reminds me of old people and respirators. Cora is bad at this. She hit my lung but not very deeply. I'll survive if I can call an ambulance.

Maybe she didn't want to kill you.

Get to the phone, make the call, then focus on breathing.

The police? You can't call the police. You'll be caught. CAUGHT!

Cora has a victim's car. A history with all the victims. You were obviously supposed to be another victim. Get to the phone.

Make the call. Focus on breathing.

I'm fading, but I manage to hoarsely call for help. The dispatcher asks me to stay on the line, but I can't focus on that. I roll on my back in my living room and struggle to breathe.

I hear sirens after a few moments. God, they're quick.

I keep thinking of how good Cora looked just before she stabbed me. How lost in her I was. That disintegrating feeling to be completely at her mercy. That fiercely bright moment where her face changed as she decided to kill me.

When the paramedics find me, I'm delirious. A bloodstained, twisted smile is frozen on my face as they load me into the ambulance. They keep asking my name, what happened, if I know who did this.

I can only whisper one name. Over and over. To them. To myself.

Cora.

The feelings are *mutual.*

Acknowledgements

To Haley, My Agent of Chaos,

I can't even fathom how I've survived without you as a PA for all these years. You're the cheese to my pizza. Without you, I'd just be sauce and dough. Which is gross. Cheese is everything. I can't breathe without cheese. I can't live without cheese. You're the cheese, and the only cheese I need. Thank you for everything, daddy.

To our Beta Readers,

Brittany, Genesis, Macie, Skarlet, Julie, Emily, Erika, Katie, Shen, Elena, and Amanda. Y'all really showed up for this one, as always. We appreciate your feedback, encouragement, and excitement for this story and these complex characters. Thank you all for being the best!

To our ARC & Hype Teams,

Slaaaaayyyyy besties! Y'all are fucking amazing. You're the bones. Without you, we'd just be flesh and blood. A meat suit with nothing to hold us together.

And to our readers, who aren't afraid to cross the line and push all boundaries when reading fiction. Make sure to drink some water and play with puppies. You deserve it after finishing this one.

Also By
Author Molly Doyle

Desires Duet

Dominant Desires

Dark Desires

Order of the Unseen Series

Scream for Us

Bloodshed

Melt for Us

About the Author

Molly Doyle has been writing since she was in grade school, and has been a published author since she was sixteen. Once she moved her talents to an online platform, her writing took off. She has reached millions of readers across the globe, with many of them crediting her for their mask kink. When she's not fantasizing about masked men, she's plotting her next erotic story.

You can reach Molly through her social media or at authormollydoyle@gmail.com.

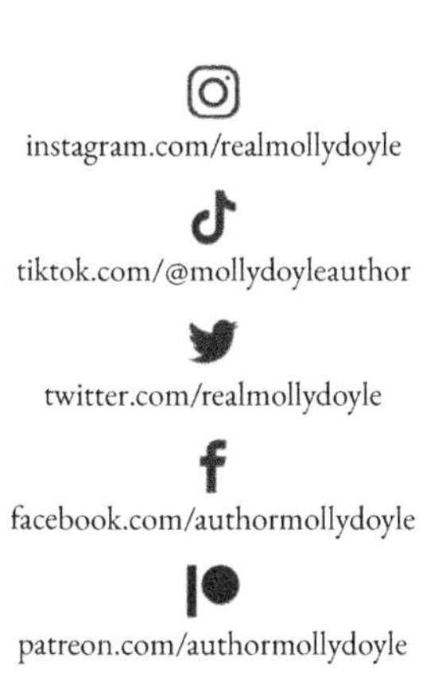

goodreads.com/authormollydoyle

amazon.com/authormollydoyle

bookbub.com/authors/molly-doyle

Printed in Great Britain
by Amazon

42942253R00158